Robert Sinker

Biographical Notes on the Librarians of Trinity College

on Sir Edward Stanhope's Foundation

Robert Sinker

Biographical Notes on the Librarians of Trinity College
on Sir Edward Stanhope's Foundation

ISBN/EAN: 9783337015756

Printed in Europe, USA, Canada, Australia, Japan

Cover: Foto ©Raphael Reischuk / pixelio.de

More available books at **www.hansebooks.com**

BIOGRAPHICAL NOTES

ON

THE LIBRARIANS

OF TRINITY COLLEGE

ON

SIR EDWARD STANHOPE'S FOUNDATION

BY

ROBERT SINKER, D.D.

LIBRARIAN OF TRINITY COLLEGE.

Cambridge:

PRINTED FOR THE CAMBRIDGE ANTIQUARIAN SOCIETY.

SOLD BY DEIGHTON, BELL, & CO.,
AND MACMILLAN & BOWES.

1897

𝕮𝖆𝖒𝖇𝖗𝖎𝖉𝖌𝖊 :

PRINTED BY J. & C. F. CLAY,

AT THE UNIVERSITY PRESS.

HENRICO MONTAGU BUTLER S.T.P.

COLLEGII SS. ET INDIV. TRINITATIS MAGISTRO

LIBELLUM DICAT

R. S.

PREFACE.

A GOOD many years ago I began filling up fragments of time by working out a complete list of my predecessors in the Librarianship of Trinity College, and adding any biographical details concerning them which came in my way. As time went on, the details grew considerably, and ultimately took form in a book, which the Cambridge Antiquarian Society is kind enough to think worth publishing. It is doubtless true that a majority of the Librarians spoken of in the following pages were little known beyond the bounds of their own College and University; still, carefully worked-out details of the past, however trifling, often have an importance indirectly to historical workers, and I am hopeful that some of the points established here may be not without their value.

Moreover, the special character of the Librarianship gives it, I think, an additional interest. It is, to the best of my belief, the only College Librarianship in either University, which forms an integral part of the foundation of its College; and further, the curious provision in the will of the founder, by which the Archbishop of Canterbury was empowered in certain cases to interpose, has more than once led to a curious history[1].

---

[1] Of course the College would necessarily require some official to take charge of the Library before the Stanhope foundation; but the Library-keeper of those earlier days was evidently merely a College servant, whose position relatively to others is amusingly shown by a Conclusion of 25 Feb. 160¾, which rules concerning payments made at graduation to "the two chief Butlers and Tonsor, the Janitor, Chapel-Clerk, and Library-Keeper."

Looking back upon so long a line of predecessors, I have ventured upon the egotism of including the present Librarian. Remembering that now, save for one short break of a few weeks, I have been a member of the foundation of my College for nearly forty years, I could not but wish to link myself on to those who had been Librarians before me.

It was suggested to me that I should begin my book with a memoir of Sir Edward Stanhope. That I have not done so, is due to no lack of respect and gratitude to my "pious founder," but simply to the fact that I have not discovered anything more about him than is contained in the short life given in Cooper's *Athenæ Cantabrigienses*[1], with its accompanying references. It is mainly thence that I draw the following brief epitome of facts.

Edward Stanhope was the fourth, or fourth surviving son of Sir Michael Stanhope, Governor of Kingston-upon-Hull (who was beheaded, 26 Feb. 155½, as an accomplice of his brother-in-law, the Lord-Protector Somerset), by his wife Anne, daughter of Nich. Rawson, Esq., of Aveley in Essex. She died 20 Feb. 158⅞. He was educated at Trinity College, and was admitted Scholar in 1560 (the College records do not give the date more minutely), Minor Fellow 23 Sept. 1564, and Major Fellow 30 April, 1566. It may be noted that he discharged the following College offices. He was Lector Græcæ Grammaticæ in 1567, Sublector quartus in 1568, Lector Linguæ Græcæ in 1570 and Thesaurarius Tertius in 1571–2. He took the degrees of B.A. 156⅔, M.A. 1566, LL.D. 1575. He supplicated for incorporation as M.A. at Oxford, 6 Sept. 1566[2], on the occasion of Elizabeth's visit, and as LL.D. on 1 Sept. 1578[3].

He was Prebendary of Botevant in York Minster from 25 Nov. 1572 until 9 Aug. 1591[4]. Among those who had held this Prebend before him were John Colet, Dean of St Paul's, and Cuthbert Tunstall, Bishop of Durham. On 5 June, 1577,

---

[1] Vol. ii., p. 470 f.
[2] Boase, *Register of the University of Oxford*, vol. i., p. 264.
[3] *Ibid.* vol. ii., part 1, p. 349.
[4] Le Neve-Hardy, vol. iii., p. 177.

he was sworn a Master in Chancery; and not later than 1578, he was appointed Chancellor of the Diocese of London. He became Vicar-General of the province of Canterbury in 1583, was Member of Parliament for Marlborough in 1586, and became Rector of Terrington in 1589. On 31 May, 1591, he was collated to the Prebend of Kentish-Town (or Cantlers) in St Paul's Cathedral[1], and, at a date subsequent to 8 Dec. 1594, he became Chancellor of that Cathedral[2], in succession to the famous Dr John Dee, who had been one of the original fellows of Trinity College. He was knighted 23 July, 1603; and died 16 March, 160⅞. He was buried in St Paul's Cathedral, and an inscription drawn up by William Camden was set up to commemorate him on the eastern wall near the great north door[3].

An extract of so much of his will as concerned his foundation at Trinity College is contained in the manuscript volume of "Wills and Charters" in the possession of Trinity College. There is also a transcript in the Baker MSS. in the British Museum[4], and a copy therefrom in the University Library[5].

Curiously enough, Sir Edward Stanhope had an elder brother, also a Sir Edward Stanhope, and the latter was one of the executors to the will of the former[6].

I must confess that the combination of lay and clerical functions in the same man and at such a date, struck me as curious—at once a rector and prebendary, and also a knight and M.P. It might indeed be said that the case is one of a lay Rector, but even so the Prebend remains. I was almost

---

[1] Le Neve-Hardy, ii. 405.

[2] *Ibid.* ii. 361.

[3] The inscription is given in Cooper's *Athenæ*, *l.c.*

[4] Baker MSS., vol. xi., pp. 334 f. (MSS. Harl., 7038).

[5] Baker MSS., D. 9, pp. 300 f. (*Cat. of MSS. in Lib. of Univ. of Camb.*, vol. v., p. 565).

[6] This duplication of names must often have caused confusion, and Mr Foster (*Alumni Oxon.* sub nom.) must be in error in speaking of Dr George Stanhope as a son of the Sir Edward Stanhope we are now considering, who seems never to have married, and who devised his estate of Wellwood to the five sons successively of his brother, Sir Edward, George being the third.

tempted to think that two Edward Stanhopes might have been "conflated" into one record, but the only other I can trace is the brother of the founder of the Librarianship, to whom I have already referred. Unfortunately, he, like his brother, was also knight and M.P.

At this stage I consulted my friend, the Rev. Dr W. Sparrow Simpson, sub-dean and librarian of St Paul's, on the chance that perhaps something in the statutes of St Paul's in force at the end of the sixteenth century might throw some light on the matter. Dr Simpson, however, tells me that there was nothing exceptional in the case of St Paul's. If indeed we are dealing here with a case of survival from pre-Reformation laxity, one can only wonder that such a survival should have been tolerated under the strong-handed rule of Elizabeth and of Whitgift.

It certainly is hard to conceive that Sir Edward Stanhope was in Holy Orders. His epitaph describes him as " in publicis Ecclesiæ et Reipublicæ negotiis versatissimus," which would hardly have been said of a cleric even of an earlier generation, without some notice of his being in Holy Orders.

Of pre-Reformation laxity there is abundance. Dr Simpson refers to the case of Colet, who was admitted to a rectory when he was only nineteen years old, when therefore he could not possibly have been in priest's orders[1]. This was in 1485, however, and there should be considerable difference between that date and 1591.

Dr Simpson kindly mentioned the matter to the Rev. George Hennessy, who is engaged in a most important work, a new edition of that part of Newcourt's *Repertorium* which refers to the beneficed clergy. Mr Hennessy states that he has met with *numerous* instances of laymen holding Prebendal stalls in St Paul's and elsewhere. These instances, however, are of pre-Reformation date[2].

---

[1] See Dr Lupton's *Life of Colet*, p. 116.

[2] For example, he mentions the case of Sir Ri. la Vache, who petitions the Pope for a Canonry of London, with expectation of a Prebend, for his son Edward, aged 13. This was granted by the Pope, 4 July, 1361. Or again, take

Mr Hennessy is inclined to think that Sir Edward Stanhope must have been in Holy Orders, though he has no proof to offer. It may be said on the one hand that the character of the rule in Church and State at the time lends support to this view; on the other hand, the wording of the epitaph and the absence of any allusion therein to the clerical office must be thought adverse evidence. I am afraid therefore that the matter must be left in abeyance.

A striking post-Reformation parallel is suggested by Dr Simpson in the person of the well-known Sir Thomas Smith, the first Regius Professor of Civil Law in this University, and Principal Secretary of State to Edward VI. and Elizabeth. Yet he was also Rector of Leverington in the Isle of Ely from 1545 to 1549; and in 1547 he was appointed Dean of Carlisle. He was deprived of the Deanery by Mary, but was restored in 1559, and retained it till his death in 1577. Certainly, however, no one would for a moment suppose from his epitaph[1] that he was in Holy Orders. Strype remarks, in connection with the appointment to the Deanery, "being at least in Deacon's Orders[2]," but he cites no evidence on the point.

It may be remembered that, at the present day, the Queen holds the first Cursal Prebend of St David's; and Dr Simpson mentions that many monarchs have been Honorary Canons in Germany.

The numerous friends, from whom I have received help in various points of detail, are all, I trust, mentioned in due

Thomas Bubbewith, who was appointed Prebendary of Wenlakesbarn in 1406, but was only ordained acolyte and sub-deacon, 17 May, 1410.

The most astonishing case mentioned by Mr Hennessy is that of James de Ispania, nephew of Queen Eleanor, who, though not ordained, was in 1306 Canon of London; who, besides several Rectories, held Canonries and Prebends in Wells, London, Dublin, Lichfield, Exeter, Sarum, York, Lincoln and elsewhere. He obtained a dispensation from Pope Boniface VIII. to hold two Rectories, the Deanery of Pontefract Castle and of St Leonard's, York, and other Canonries and Prebends, not being ordained priest. James de Ispania was absolutely a layman, not even in any of the minor Orders.

[1] See Strype's *Life of Sir Thomas Smith*, p. 152, ed. Oxford, 1820: Cooper's *Athenæ*, i. 372.

[2] *op. cit.*, p. 31.

course.   To two successive Registraries of the University, the
late Rev. Dr Luard, and Mr J. W. Clark, my especial thanks
are due.   The latter has allowed me to inflict upon him
questions on a multiplicity of details, in a way which many
men would call ἀναίδεια, and has helped me to clear up many
doubtful points.   Since the manuscript of my work was transcribed for the press, the Archbishop of Canterbury and the
Bishop of St David's, to both of whom my thanks were due
(pp. 7, 35), have passed away.

In conclusion, I wish to remark that in a work of this kind,
where a large number of small details are drawn together from
a variety of sources, I am keenly alive to the paramount need of
accuracy and the difficulty of securing it; though I believe I
have taken all possible pains.   In the Preface to my Catalogue
of the *Incunabula* in the College Library, published in 1876,
I referred to the difficulty of securing accuracy in bibliographical work, which is full of like perils.   Certainly a further
experience of twenty-one years has taught me how hard it is,
spite of all pains, to avoid error.

R. S.

TRINITY COLLEGE,
    24th February, 1897.

LIBRARIANS OF TRINITY COLLEGE.

LIBRARIANS OF TRINITY COLLEGE

SIR EDWARD STANHOPE'S FOUNDATION.

(I.) WILLIAM HICKES. [1609–1611½.]

Sir Edward Stanhope died 16 March, 160⅞, and his will, which was dated 28 February, 160⅔, was proved 25 March, 1608. In this he bequeathed £700 to Trinity College, to buy lands for the maintenance of a Library-Keeper and Under-Library-Keeper, and most minute directions are therein given as to the conditions of election and the tenure of office. Among other things he ruled that the Library-Keeper was to be chosen "within one Fortnight of the receipte of the foresaid £700 or within one Fortnight after my Funerall, if the Librarie[1] be finished before my death: and that my Executors be tyed to the paiment of the first yeares annuitie of £30." Yet there seems to have been some little delay.

The first person appointed on this Foundation was William Hickes (or Hicks). I can find no record of his election in the Conclusion Book, nor of his admission as Librarian in any of the Admission Books; yet he must have been appointed about Lady-Day, 160⅔, for in the Senior Bursar's book for the year

---

[1] This is of course the old Library in the north-west angle of the Old Court. The range of which it forms part must have been finished between 1599 and 1601 (Willis-Clark, *Architectural History of the University of Cambridge*, vol. ii. p. 481).

ending Michaelmas, 1609, Mr Hickes receives two quarters' stipend.

Although no Christian name is given, it was certainly William Hickes (B.A., 160⅜; M.A., 1609), since there had been no other of the name at Trinity, since Henry Hicks (B.A., 15⁶⁸⁄₇₈), who would not only have been too old, but had never proceeded to M.A. William Hickes was admitted scholar 12 April, 1605, at the same election with Giles Fletcher.

I think it is possible that it was this William Hickes who was collated Prebendary of Bedford Magna in Lincoln Cathedral, 20 Aug., 1612[1] (installed 23 Aug.); and whether there be any connection between the two events or no, it will be noticed that the vacancy in the Librarianship and the appointment to the Lincoln Prebend both took place in 1612. In any case, the Lincoln Prebendary must either have been our Librarian, or the Oxford man of the same name mentioned below. There is only one person from each University who satisfies the conditions. I had hoped that the Lincoln Chapter Records might mention the University, but my friend Chancellor Leeke tells me that the only note to the name of the new prebendary is "artium magister." If he were not the Librarian, he must have been an Oxford man (B.A. 158¼, from Brasenose : M.A. 1584, from Magdalen : Chaplain of Magdalen, 1585-9)[2], whose age perhaps makes him more likely.

A person of the name was Vicar of Edmonton in 1589.

Prebendary William Hickes, be he which he may of the two, was on 7 Dec. 1625 inducted as Rector of Stoke-Hammond in Buckinghamshire[3], a living once held by good Bishop Hacket. I thought it possible that the doubt as to the University might have been cleared up by a memorial tablet in the church, but the present Rector of Stoke-Hammond, the Rev. E. Pain, informs me that there is none, nor is there any record of his burial. He sends me, however, a note of the marriage of the Rector's

---

[1] Le Neve-Hardy, *Fasti Ecclesiæ Anglicanæ*, vol. ii. p. 108.

[2] Foster, *Alumni Oxon.* sub nom.

[3] Lipscomb, *History and Antiquities of the County of Buckingham*, iv. 362. Lipscomb adds, "He died about 1645." The date was actually 1646 (Le Neve-Hardy, *l.c.*).

daughter, where the date may perhaps be thought to be somewhat in favour of our fixing upon the older man[1].

There was another William Hickes of Trinity (B.A. 164½, M.A. 1645), who might be the son of the Librarian. A William Hickes, born at Oundle, 13 April, 1647, eldest son of "William Hickes, M.A." (not improbably the preceding) was admitted at Merchant Taylors' School in 1657–8[2].

One of the name was Rector of Tortworth, Gloucestershire, in 1644[3].

(II.) Nicholas Parker. [161½–1625.]

On 19 Feb. 161½, the entry occurs in the Conclusion Book, "This 19th of February, the Library Keeper's place was granted to Ds Parker." Again no Christian name is given, but the only member of the College named Parker, then a B.A., was Nicholas Parker[4]. He took the degrees of B.A. 160⁸⁄₉, and M.A. 1612. He was admitted scholar 22 April, 1608; and on 22 Sept. 1610, Sir Parker and Sir Baker were chosen "conducts potentia," that is, were elected not to fill up actual vacancies among the chaplains, but vacancies which might subsequently arise. On 23 Dec. 1614, Mr Parker was granted by the Master and Seniors, a Paling (or Palin) Exhibition of £4, which he held as long as he was Librarian.

The system of pre-election was often applied to the Chaplains; we now find it in the case of the Librarianship, for on 9 March, 161⁴⁄₅, we read in the Conclusion Book, "concluded that Sr Stoakes[5] shall be Library Keeper upon the next vacancy of the place." However, no vacancy occurred for nearly ten years, and then, if I read the circumstances aright, it is con-

[1] Catherine, daughter of William Hickes, the Rector, was married to Walter Pake, on 2 February, 1628, that is presumably 162⁸⁄₉.

[2] Robinson, *Register of Merchant Taylors' School*, p. 241.

[3] Foster, *Alumni Oxon.* sub nom.

[4] Before him was Samuel Parker, M.A. 1596, whose degree cuts him out, and after him is none till John Parker, B.A. 1628.

[5] This must be David Stokes, admitted Scholar, 5 April, 1611, B.A. 161⁴⁄₅, afterwards Fellow of Peterhouse, M.A. 1618, D.D. 1630, incorporated at Oxford, 1645. See Welch, *Alumni West.* p. 80; Foster, *Alumni Oxon.* sub nom.

nected with a very curious line of procedure on the part of the College.

Three meetings of the Seniority took place in September, 1625. At the first of these (Sept. 3), Mr Parker has letters of Attorney to compound the matters between the College and the sequestrators of Aysgarth. At the second (Sept. 16), Will. Short was sent in Mr Parker's place, "being lately dead on his journey into Yorkshire," for dispatch of the same business of Aysgarth. At the third (Sept. 19), the Palin Exhibition which "Mr Parker the Librarian" had held was filled up, and a new Librarian was also chosen. Now while one cannot see on what principle the College should choose its Librarian to arrange College business in Yorkshire, still having regard to the sequence of events in the three September Seniorities, and to the fact that there was no other member of the Foundation of the College at that time named Parker, we can hardly doubt that, be the explanation what it may, it was Mr Parker the Librarian who was so sent. He may himself have been personally connected with Aysgarth, but we have no evidence of this.

(III.) PETER HERSENT. [1625–1631.]

As we have already said, the new Librarian was elected on 19 September, 1625. The entry in the Conclusion Book runs as follows, "At the same meeting Mr Hairsant was chosen into the Library Keeper's place, which Mr Parker before him held; submitting himselfe to those lawes and orders which are mentioned in Sir Edward Stanhope's will and such others as the Master and 8 Seniors from time to time should agree upon and think fitt to make for the ordering of the Library and better use of the Books therein."

We now have got a person of a less shadowy personality than his two predecessors. Peter Hersent had been educated at Westminster, was elected thence to Cambridge in 1616[1], and was admitted, with one other, Scholar of Trinity, on 2 May, 1617.

---

[1] Welch. *Alumni West.* p. 85.

He took his B.A. in 162$\frac{0}{1}$, and his M.A. in 1624. He appears to have been a somewhat turbulent person, in the light of the statement signed by him among the Admonitions at the end of a book of Admission of Fellows, etc.:—" Februarij 22, 1621. Wheras I haue verie vnadvisedly and rashly strucken one Mr. Halfhead, Manciple of o^r Colledg, to the *shedding of blood* [endaundgering of his eye[1]], I doe acknowledg myself to haue receiued an admonition for that fault tending to expulsion. Peter Hersent." It will be seen that at this time Peter Hersent was a Bachelor Scholar of the College, and with him was implicated one Thomas Shirley, who makes the same apology. The latter culprit was somewhat the older. He[2] had taken the degrees of B.A. 161$\frac{7}{8}$ and M.A. 1619, and was elected Minor Fellow in 1618. We thus actually have a regent Master and Fellow of the College behaving in this outrageous way.

Hersent's election to the Librarianship on Sept. 19 was followed by his admission on Sept. 24. The entry in the Admission Book, rather fuller than the ordinary curt form, runs, " Ego Petrus Hersent admissus fui et juratus custos Bibliothecæ a Dno. Edvardo Stanhop fundatæ in præsentia magistri et octo seniorum."

At the election to the Chancellorship of the University, 1 June, 1626, " Pet. Harsnet" voted for the Duke of Buckingham[3].

Mr Hersent was incorporated at Oxford, 5 June, 1628[4]. There was another Peter Hersent at Oxford (Queen's College, B.A. 1705), who may have been the grandson of the foregoing[5].

---

[1] The words in italics are crossed out in the original, and the words in brackets are written above them.

[2] It was Mr Shirley who succeeded to Mr Parker's Palin Exhibition. He hanged himself in April, 1637. The story is told in the Baker MSS. D, § 9, 21 (*Cat. of MSS. in Lib. of Univ. of Camb.* v. 565). Baker had extracted the story of the suicide from a letter of the Rev. G. Garrard to Lord Strafford, written 28 April, 1637 (*Strafford Letters*, ii. 72). Mr Garrard speaks of Shirley as a Bachelor of Divinity, but there is no trace of this degree to be found in the Registry.

[3] List in University Registry, printed in Cooper's *Annals*, iii. 186 f.

[4] Foster, *Alumni Oxon.* sub nom.

[5] *Ibid.*

In *Gratulatio Academiae Cantabrigiensis de Serenissimi Principis reditu ex Hispanijs exoptatissimo* (Cantab. 1623), are elegiacs (p. 34) signed by P.H., C.T. These are probably by Peter Hersent.

Cole's MSS. xlv. 235, 261. Welch, *Alumni West.* p. 85.

(IV.)   WILLIAM CLUTTERBOOKE[1].   [1631–1641.]

The new Librarian, like his predecessor, was from Westminster, whence he was elected to Cambridge in 1623[2], and was admitted scholar of Trinity, 9 April, 1624[3]. He took the degrees of B.A. 162⅚, M.A. 1631. B.D. 1640. He was elected Librarian 21 April, 1631, and admitted on April 27. The Conclusion Book does not directly record his election, nor do I find his admission in the Admission Book, but perhaps the following entry in the Conclusion Book may be meant to cover the latter:—"April 27, 1631. It was agreed that Mr Clutterbooke, who was chosen Librarie Keeper in Mr Hersent's place the 21st of Aprill, should be admitted this day; and so he was." We catch a stray glimpse of him once again a few months after his election. In the Conclusion of Jan. 26, 163½, we read, "granted at the same time to...Mr Clotterbooke to be in extra commons with allowance of...6ˢ 8ᵈ." This would, I suppose, presumably point to an illness.

He was one of the writers of complimentary verses, prefixed to Duport's *Liber Job Graeco carmine redditus* (Cantab. 1637); and has three sets of verses in the *Carmen Natulitium* (Cantab. 1635), two sets in the Συνῳδία (Cantab. 1637), and two sets in the *Voces Votivae* (Cantab. 1640). In the first three of these books he gives his name as Clotterbook, in the last he signs himself, Guliel. Clutterbooke, S.T.B. Coll. Trin.

---

[1] Also Clotterbook, Clotterbooke. The spelling at the head of the section is that in which his appointment to the Librarianship is recorded.

[2] *Alumni West.* p. 93. A John Clutterbuck, possibly the brother of the present, was elected to Oxford from Westminster in 1616 (*ibid.* p. 85).

[3] Another of the scholars at this admission was Thomas Randolph, the well-known poet.

A curious incident has to be recorded in connection with the year 1638. According to Sir Edward Stanhope's will, if the Librarianship became vacant in any way, or if the Librarian had in any way forfeited his office, the Master and Seniors must fill up the vacant post within fourteen days or the presentation was to lapse to the Archbishop of Canterbury. A certain Samuel Turbervile[1], a young graduate of the College, apparently on the look-out for promotion for himself, maintained in 1638 that from various causes Mr Clutterbuck had forfeited his post, and ultimately Archbishop Laud, accepting this view, claimed the next presentation.

Of the correspondence which ensued, Mr Aldis Wright could find, when Senior Bursar, no trace in the Muniment Room of Trinity College; but I have found draughts of two letters in the Lambeth Library, one from Laud to the College, and the other the answer of the College. Of each of these there are three several draughts, inserted amid the correspondence between Archbishop Wake and Bentley on the occasion of a similar dispute in 1728 [Lamb. 1156]. So far as I am aware, neither of these documents has ever been printed, and I accordingly reproduce them here by the permission of the Archbishop of Canterbury.

One of the draughts [no. 4] is in the opinion of my friend, Mr Kershaw, the Lambeth Librarian, in Laud's own handwriting. It contains both letters, that of Laud to the College, and the answer, on the same sheet of paper, as though it were desired to keep the correspondence together for convenience of reference. The second draught [no. 4 *bis*] contains a certain amount of additional matter in the answer of the College, and it is this form of the answer therefore which I have subjoined, noting one or two minor differences, other than those of mere

---

[1] Samuel Turbervile took the degrees of B.A. 163¾, and M.A. 1637. He was the author of verses in *Ducis Eboracensis Fasciae* (Cantab. 1633), and in Συνῳδία, *Sive Musarum Cantabrigiensium Concentus et Congratulatio* (Cantab. 1637). He is perhaps the same Turbervile who was appointed chorister of the College, 28 March, 1632. He had not been a scholar of the College, and therefore his appointment to the Librarianship would have been in defiance of Sir Edw. Stanhope's will.

spelling. The third draught of the letter of the College is a transcript in Bentley's writing [no. 43[1]]. The original, however, from which he transcribed it, can, as I have said, no longer be found in the College Muniment Room.

(1) Archbishop Laud to the Master (Dr Comber) and Seniors of Trinity College[2].

S. in X[m].

After my hearty commendations etc. I am informed that the orders set down and appointed by Sir Edw: Stanhope, Kn[t] & D[r] of Laws (a worthy Benefactor to y[e] House) for the Practice & Reglement of yo[r] Library-Keeper, have not been observed by him,; where upon your[3] Disposing of that place is devolved to me, as by the last Will and Testament of the s[d] Kn[t] deceased you may plainly[4] perceyve. These are therefore to pray & require you to give me a present accompt of this business, & if the Information here mentioned be true, I shall expect that you fail not likewise to send me the names of some discreet & able young men of your Colledge, whom you conceive fittest for such an Employment, that thereupon I may make Choice of some one of them, & see him presently settled accordingly. So having nothing else to trouble you with[5] at this time, I leave you to God's blessed Protection & Rest.

Your very loving Friend

W. Cant.

Lambeth, Nov. 28, 1638.

(2) The Master and Seniors of Trinity College to Archbishop Laud[6].

May it please yo[r] Grace ;

Having received yo[r] Grace's Letter concerning our Library-Keeper's

[1] This transcript is referred to in a letter of Bentley to Archbishop Wake, 15 Dec. 1728, "The rough Draught of the College's Answer to Archbishop Laud, which could not be found when Dr Thomas Bentley drew up his Argument, has yesterday been found in a Box of our Registry; and I thought it my duty to copy it out and send it to your Grace the first opportunity..." (*Correspondence of R. Bentley, D.D.*, p. 693).

[2] This follows Laud's draught. I note the variations of what I have called the "second draught," other than varieties of spelling.

[3] "the."

[4] *Add* "and fully."

[5] *Omit.*

[6] Here for the reason given above, I have followed the wording of what I have called the "second draught," noting the variations in the copy in Laud's writing. For a subsequent use of the fact of this double recension, see *Bentley Correspondence*, p. 696.

Office being devolved to yo' Grace's Election ; we according to the Tenor of yo' Grace's Letter requiring of us to be Inform'd of the true Estate of that Matter, return you our opinion and judgment, as we concieved before your Grace's Letter having had the same Inducement : most humbly submitting the same to yo' Grace's better Interpretation.

May it please yo' Grace

There came to us one Mr Turberville, sometime a Member of our Society, who accused to us the Library Keeper of Loss of his place, & was likewise Petitioner to be Elected thereto.

His Articles ag* : Him were four :

1. That he had accepted the Office of Poser in the University, contrary to a clause in the Benefactor's Will, forbidding him on Loss of Place, ipso facto, to accept of any office.

2. That he had read a certain Lecture in the College Hall for a Friend (& who had another for his Deputy) contrary to some Words in the same clause.

3. For not Keeping his Exits & Redits, by which the time of his Continuance, strictly limited, might appear.

4. For that he had procured a Dispensation from the King's Majesty to take the Degree of Batchelor in Divinity, which Degree by the Will is prohibited to him.

May it please yo' Grace,

Having met together more than once for the discussing of these Articles ; and using the best Advice of our Lawyers which this Term tyme were left at home, we conceived, humbly submitting to y' Gr: Judgment,

That the Poser's Place is no Office—being a work but of two Days, but an Assistance[1] only to the Proctors, as app' : by the words of the University Statute & Proctor's Book P.... and by a Register'd Grace in the University so calling it.   Else also the Proctors to whom they are Assistant would be said also to take an office.

For reading for his Friend in the Hall we likewise with Submission conceived that it being not for himself, but as Deputy, was no breach of the same clause voiding his place, inasmuch as we see both by our Statutes, and by daily pract* : that such persons [who are not capable of some offices in their own Persons are appointed & may execute the same offices[2]] for another in that place.

[1] "Assistant."

[2] A note is appended in the "second draught" in a line with the text, on the blank space at the right hand of the column:—"These words are so defaced in

For the not keeping his Exits & Redits by wch his Continuance & Discontinuance must be known, we see not that any penalty is expressed in the Will, but conceive it is left to the Master & Seniors censuring [1], of which there is mention in the same Will, pag...., neither did it appear to us that he had been absent above his Days allow'd, for want of his Exits & Redits, for which we gave him a Censure, & he alleged his absence was in time of publick Calamity, which is excepted in the Will itself.

And last of all, for procuring a Dispensation to take a Degree contrary to the Will, we know not that Sr Edw: Stanhope's Will can hinder the King's prerogative in his own Foundation. Besides that, the said Dispensation was never used.

[One thing more we humbly crave Pardon to speak not in our own regard, but for the Right of the College in succession. It is conceived by our Council that tho' this place shou'd by any default be forfieted ipso facto, yet a declaratory sentence is required before absolute Voydance, as we see it practised in like Cases, & as it may seem touched P.... of the Will. And that that Declaratory Sentence of Voydance belongeth to the Master & Seniors upon Notice—and by consequence there is no Devolution unless a Choice be not made or agreed upon in 14 days after such voidance [2].]

Your Grace's offer is most Favourable, and we desire not to decline yo': Grace's Election, but humbly submit ourselves to yo' Grace's judgment and better Interpretation. And if your Grace be not therewithal satisfied we shall be ready to admit of such a person as yo' Grace shall commend to us."

What the further course of this controversy was, I am quite

the Original, wch is torn & but a rough Draught that they are here supply'd by conjecture." The bracket and its contents are not in Laud's draught, but a space is left.

[1] "concerning of which."

[2] In the "second draught" a note is appended in the blank space on the left:—"These words between these [ ] are cross'd out & probably, on deliberation of the M^r and Sen^rs were omitted." In Laud's draught, the upper part of the second half of the sheet, where the words in brackets would have come, has been cut off. In Bentley's draught the brackets are not found, and the concluding paragraph of the letter, "your Grace's offer...," is omitted. In his letter to the Archbishop of 31 Dec. 1728 (*Bentley Corresp.* p. 697) Bentley declares that, in the Draught from which he copied it, this last paragraph was crossed out, as evidently not consonant with the views of the Seniority when the letter was sent. Clearly there is a Bentleian and an anti-Bentleian recension, so to speak, and one can hardly doubt that there must have been unfair dealing on the part of one side or other. In the absence, however, of all trace of the original, it seems impossible to arrive at the truth. Yet Bentley's letter above referred to declares that the cancelling of which he speaks has been seen by the Master *and Seniors*.

unable to say. Whether the Archbishop was convinced by the arguments of the Master and Seniors, or whether the influence which had got Clutterbuck his dispensation stood him in further good stead, or whether the increasing civil troubles gave Laud weightier matters to think of,—at any rate in spite of the humble surrender by the College, Clutterbuck remained Librarian for more than three years after the date of the Archbishop's letter given above, and took the degree of B.D. for which he had obtained the Dispensation[1].

This document is thus indexed in the College Register— "King's letter allowing William Clotterbooke, Master of Arts and Library Keeper, to take his Degree of Bachelor of Divinity." It is thus endorsed, "By virtue of his Ma^{tie's} letters above written and now red before the Master and Seniors they gave leave to Mr Clutterbooke to take his degree of Bachelor of Divinitie without p'iudice to his place. 19 September, 1638."

Clutterbuck signed the declaration in the Registrary's book, required before taking the degree of B.D., on 10 (or 11[2]) June, 1640, so that the degree was presumably taken on St Barnabas's Day. One of the preliminaries for this degree, until recent years, was the preaching of a Latin Sermon before the University (*Concio ad Clerum*). It is this which is referred to in the curiously worded Conclusion of 10 Jan. 1639 (i.e. 16$\frac{38}{49}$);— "This day leave was given to Mr Clutterbooke to *Clerum*, by the Master and 8 Seniors."

---

[1] An apparent allusion to this affair occurs in a short letter of Laud to Trinity College, a transcript of which is given in the Letter Book of Dr Henry Smyth (Master of Magdalene, 1626–42, and Vice-Chancellor, 1635–36). It is dated 10 Dec. 1638, and superscribed in a different hand, "To Trin. Coll. about the Library Keeper's place." It runs, "I doe desire you to be very carefull of the observance of those thinges which are given you by the will or other ordinance of any benefactors; for if that be not done it will disharten other well minded men to doe that for Colledges wch they would otherwise have beene easilie induced to doe. So wishing all prosperouse successe to your selfe and that whole Society, I leave you to God's blessed protection and rest. Your lovinge friend, W. Cant." (Patrick MSS. vol. xxiii. § 1: see *Cat. of MSS. in the Library of the Univ. of Camb.* vol. v. p. 173.) This, however, throws no further light on the history of the affair.

[2] The writing appears doubtful.

I cannot doubt that it was this William Clutterbuck who became Rector of Wodeham Ferrers (Essex) in 1641, and of Danbury (Essex) in 1662. Both of these livings were in the gift of Sir Humphrey Mildmay and both were vacated by Clutterbuck's death in 1665. I learn through the kindness of the Rev. Charles P. Plumptre, Rector of Wodeham (or Woodham) Ferrers, and the Rev. John B. Plumptre, Rector of Danbury, that there is no memorial of any kind, tablet, window, or the like, of Clutterbuck, in either church.

There was a Laurence Clutterbuck at Trinity, B.A. 166⅝, who might be the son of the foregoing.

Cole's MSS. xlv. 262. Welch, *Alumni West.* p. 93.
.Newcourt, *Reg. Eccl.* ii. 205, 682.
White Kennett, *Reg. and Chron.* 789.

(V.) THOMAS GRIFFITH. [1641–167⅔.]

In the case of this Librarian I have met with a difficulty, which I have utterly failed to solve, in spite of much help from two successive Registraries, Dr Luard and Mr J. W. Clark, who most kindly took the utmost pains in the matter, but to no purpose.

The former gave me a note of the M.A. degree of Thomas Griffith in 1639, adding that he ought to be a B.A. of 163⅝, but that of this degree there was no trace. Feeling bound to offer a theory, I suggested (1) that there was some *lacuna* in the B.A. list, or (2) that Griffith was incorporated from Oxford, or (3) that he was granted the M.A. degree by Royal Mandate. It turned out, however, that there was no *lacuna* in the MS., and the absence of the note *Oxoniensis* or *per Litteras Regias* seemed to be conclusive against the other ideas. I felt therefore forced to give the matter up as an unsolved puzzle, and accounted for the irregularity by the troublous condition of England at the time.

A year or two ago, when working through some volumes of Cole's MSS. in the British Museum, I came upon a list of the Westminster Scholars elected to Trinity. Under the year

1632 occurred the entry "Thomas Mutton *als* Griffith[1]." Assuming for the present this *alias* to be correct, we have everything dovetailing together perfectly.

Thomas Mutton was educated at Westminster, was elected to Cambridge in 1632[2], was admitted Westminster scholar of Trinity, 3 May, 1633, and took his B.A. degree in 163⅚, no M.A. being recorded, corresponding to the absence of a B.A. for Griffith. Doubtless Cole had due warrant for the *alias*, but where he got his information from I cannot in the least say.

Dr Rutherford, the Head Master of Westminster School, kindly informs me that there is nothing in the records under his care which casts the least light upon it, while the books of Trinity College and of the University Registry seem alike to offer us two disjointed halves, not making a whole.

It then occurred to me that, assuming with Cole that the two names belonged to one person, it was possible that he shifted from the use of one name to the other between his B.A. and M.A. degrees, and thus in the list of the scholars given from year to year in the Senior Bursar's book as receiving payment the change would be visible. Unfortunately, while in the Senior Bursar's book for the year ending Michaelmas, 1637, the name of Ds Mutton occurs in its place, so that the evidence, if anywhere, is to be looked for in the two succeeding volumes, we are suddenly pulled up by finding that the volumes for these two years are wanting and that the series goes on again with the volume for the year ending with Michaelmas, 1640. I must therefore leave the matter for the present unsolved, merely repeating that Cole must obviously have had some evidence, though unfortunately I am quite unable to get at it. I should add that Mr J. W. Clark most kindly had tracings made for me of the signatures of Thomas Mutton at his B.A. degree in 1636, and of Thomas Griffith at his M.A. in 1639, and I cannot honestly say that they bear any particular resemblance to one another.

Thomas Griffith became Librarian in 1641. There is no

---

[1] Cole's MSS. vol. xlv. 263.
[2] *Alumni West.* p. 104.

reference to his election in the Conclusion Book, but his admission is recorded on Dec. 15 of that year:—"Thomas Griffith iuratus et admissus in officium Bibliothecarium (*sic*) hujus Collegij." Just as his earlier history forms an awkward puzzle, so in a few years after his appointment we are faced with a second puzzle of a different kind. In a Conclusion of 15 October, 1645, it is ruled, "Agreed then by the Master and present Seniority that Mr Archer[1] be required to deliver up the key of the Library for Sir Davies[2] and that he shall have the wages for the present, which is due quarterly to the Library Keeper."

What had become of Griffith and how Mr Archer came to be holding the key of the Library, I am quite unable to say. Possibly, amid the civil troubles of the time, Griffith may have left Cambridge, as the Conclusion of 19 June, 1646, suggests, and the king's letter in his behalf in 1666 would show on which of the two sides Griffith would range himself. If the key were delivered to Sir Davies, it will be seen that he did not hold it long. A Conclusion of 19 June, 1646, runs, "Then agreed by the Master and Seniors that Mr Griffith be wholly removed from the Library Keeper's place, for his long neglect thereof, etc.,"

[1] Mr Archer was doubtless the Thomas Archer who was entered a member of Trinity College, 9 July, 1635; B.A. $16\frac{38}{39}$; M.A. 1643. The only other Archer of Trinity at all about this time was Anthony Archer, admitted Jan. 29, $163\frac{4}{5}$, but he does not seem to have taken a degree.

[2] It does not seem possible to identify this Davies with certainty. There was no scholar of the College of that name at the time, but on 27 October, 1645, "Sir Davies, Oxoniensis" was admitted under Mr Bradshaw; and by an order of Parliament, 23 Feb. $164\frac{5}{6}$, Sir Davies and seven others are admitted into eight vacant Fellowships. On 2 March, $164\frac{5}{6}$, Sir Davies has the Civil Law Fellowship given to him. On 7 March, $164\frac{5}{6}$, the College sanctioned the Grace for M.A. for Sir Davies [John Davies]. The University Register shows that on 22 April, 1646, John Davies is admitted to the same degree here as at Oxford (I presume as a necessary preliminary before proceeding to M.A.). Mr Davies, presumably the same person, was made Hebrew Lecturer at Trinity, 21 Sept. 1648, and became a Senior in 1649. It is not clear what is the Oxford record of Sir Davies. The person who seems to fit in best is the John Davies admitted at Queen's 10 Sept. 1636, B.A. (from Balliol) 25 June, 1640; the only other possible one being one who took his B.A. from New College, 18 Dec. 1634. I learn through the kindness of the Rev. T. V. Bayne, Keeper of the Archives, that there is no note in the Oxford Register as to whether either of these men migrated to Cambridge.

and in one of 2 July following we read, "Then agreed that Sir Holloway[1] should be elected into yᵉ Library Keeper's place, who was afterwards upon the taking of his oath, admitted."

The Conclusion of 19 June was subsequently erased, and, in that of 2 July, the name of Sir Holloway was crossed out. As a matter of fact, things must soon have righted themselves, for, while Holloway receives the Librarian's stipend in 1646, yet thenceforward Griffith receives it till his death.

Besides being Librarian, Griffith, like John Laughton and Clagett after him, was a "Tutor" of the College[2]; the earliest instance of a pupil entered under him which I have noticed being of 10 March, 164$\frac{8}{9}$, and the latest 11 March, 165$\frac{3}{4}$.

After the stormy commencement, Griffith appears thenceforward in tranquil guise, and in so critical a year as 1649, we find (11 May) a Conclusion, "Then also given to Mʳ Griffith, Library Keeper, tenne pounds," no reason being stated. We find a passing allusion to extra work done in the Library in aid of the Librarian and Under-Librarian, the latter of whom would at that time vacate his office on taking his B.A. degree:— March 21, 164$\frac{9}{50}$, "It is concluded that five pounds be given to Sir Pockley[3] as a gratuity, he having done something which is usefull in the Library."

---

[1] Thomas Holloway was B.A. in 164$\frac{4}{5}$, M.A. 1649. He was made Lady Elwis's Exhibitioner, 28 Jan. 164$\frac{5}{6}$. On 5 Nov. 1647, he was one of three appointed chaplains, though he does not appear in the Senior Bursar's book as such till 1649.

[2] It is true that this might be "Mʳ Griffiths the fellowe" [so named in a Conclusion of 4 Dec. 1646], but I do not think that this is likely. The Fellow in question must have been George Griffith, socius minor in 1645, as there is no other one of the name at all near this time. But George Griffith never holds any of the offices discharged by all resident fellows, and so passes out of sight. Nor does the University Register furnish any help. All that we find there is as follows: a George Griffith from Oxford takes his M.A. in 1645 (there is no B.A. to correspond) and a Griffith (christian name not stated) took his B.A. and LL.B. in 164$\frac{4}{5}$ from Queens' and his M.A. in 1647. He died 6 Jan. 168$\frac{8}{9}$, ætat. 64.

[3] Thomas Pockley (Eboracensis) was entered as sub-sizar under Mr Rolls, 12 March, 164$\frac{8}{9}$; admitted scholar, 13 April, 1649; fellow, 29 Sept. 1650. He has leave given to travel "with college seal, and have traveller's expenses, when Mʳ Rich's time is up, if no one senior to him claims it," 19 Jan. 165$\frac{2}{3}$. On the following 24 March, the patent is sealed, and three years' leave given.

The next entry (3 Sept. 1657) refers, I should presume, to the grant by Sir Edward Stanhope, but if so, I am quite unaware what should have called for such a transcription at this time. The Conclusion of the above date runs :—" Ordered that the Senior Bursar pay twentie nobles to Mr Griffith for writing and examining a copie of the founder's Originall grant, and a marke to Mr Nealand for examining and binding it ; provided that they doe together with the Register (sic) exactly examine it over againe."

In 1659, Mrs Elizabeth Peyton, widow, left legacies to her friends Mr Thomas Griffith and three others, all of Trinity College[1].

From time to time Griffith's name occurs in the Conclusion Book in connection with statements of dividend; and, on 11 Dec. 1662, the Senior Bursar is directed to pay Mr Griffith the sum of £8. 4s. 4½d., the reason not stated.

However, on the next occasion of a special gift to him, there was a very definite reason. In the winter of 166$ (I am unaware of the exact date), the Library roof was destroyed by a fire, which also probably damaged the walls[2], a fact which was doubtless not without influence in aiding the project for building a new and larger Library, which however was not taken in hand till the time of the succeeding Master, Dr Barrow. The nearest approximation I can give to the date of the fire is that furnished by a Conclusion of 12 Jan. 166$, recognizing the special care which had devolved on the Librarian :—

" Agreed then by the Master and Seniors that ten pounds be given and payd by the Bursar to Mr Griffith for his charges and paines extraordinary in the Library upon the firing of it and since."

We spoke above of political feeling possibly having some influence on Griffith's career. Sir Edward Stanhope had been very emphatic in ruling that his Librarian should in no case hold any other post—" office, lecture, preferment, or preachershipp... but the verie firste acceptaunce of anie of these Functions shall

---

[1] Waters, *The Chesters of Chicheley*, p. 318.
[2] Willis-Clark, ii. 531.

presently disable him from continuing the place of Library Keeper." Yet, in spite of this, we have at a Seniority on 22 Oct. 1666 the Conclusion, "Agreed then that Mr Thomas Griffith be chosen Register (*sic*) in the place of Mr Rhodes." The irregularity is explained by a subsequent Conclusion of Nov. 8:

"Ordered then by the Master and Seniors that his maiesties Letters in behalf of Mr Griffith be entered and accepted, and that Mr Griffith be continued in both places of Library Keeper and Register (*sic*) accordingly." This, I suppose, favours the idea that Griffith's political views may have had some bearing on the incidents referred to under 1645 and 1646.

Griffith held both posts to his death, nearly eight years later. Alderman Newton, who succeeded him as Registrar, records in his Diary, "Mr Thomas Griffith of Trinity Colledge in Cambridge dyed on Saturday morning at London the 21st March 1673 [i.e. 167¾] *about 3 of the clock*[1]."

NOTE.

Since the above section was written, I have learnt some facts, through the kindness of the Rev. Thomas Williams, Rector of Aston Clinton, Buckinghamshire, which may possibly explain the curious *alias* I have referred to in connection with Thomas Griffith.

From him I learn that Eleanor Williams, daughter of — Williams of Conway, married as her first husband Evan Griffiths of Pengwern, and bore him three sons, Robert, John and Thomas. Evan Griffiths died in 1616, and his widow subsequently married Sir Peter Mytton (or Mutton)[2], Chief Justice of North Wales, and bore him two daughters. Sir Peter died in 1637.

Mr Williams considers that there is reason for supposing that Evan Griffiths died young and that his three boys would thus be under the tutelage of their step-father.

---

[1] *Diary*, p. 71: in publications of Cambridge Antiquarian Society.

[2] See Foster's *Alumni Oxon.* sub nom. It will be remembered that the name Mytton, *according to Welsh pronunciation*, would be identical with the English word Mutton.

Is it not then conceivable that they may in a loose sort of way have borne their step-father's surname? If then we assume that the Thomas Mutton who took his B.A. in 163⅜ is the same with the Thomas Griffith who took his M.A. in 1639, and the same also with the Thomas Griffiths of the above note, the difficulty is explained.

The date of Evan Griffiths' death, taken in conjunction with the date of Thomas Griffith's B.A. in 163⅜, shews that Thomas must have been a baby or a very young child at his father's death. On his mother changing her name by re-marriage, the three young boys may have been currently styled by the new name, and by this name, we may suppose, Thomas passes through his school life at Westminster and his early years at Cambridge. Indeed he does not assume his true paternal name until after his step-father's death.

Whether this suggestion be well-founded or not, it seems to me to be at any rate far from improbable.

(VI.) JAMES MANFEILD. [167¾—1679.]

Thomas Griffith had died on March 21, and on March 24 his successor James Manfeild[1] was appointed. The new Librarian had been educated at St Paul's School, coming thence as an exhibitioner to Trinity[2]. Here he was entered as a sizar, 20 February, 166⅔, under Mr Pulleyn, Isaac Newton's tutor, was chosen into an unnamed Exhibition on 22 October, 1666, and was admitted Scholar, 17 April, 1668, on the same day with John Laughton, who succeeded him as Librarian.

He took the degrees of B.A. in 166⅔, and of M.A. in 1672, and it will thus be seen either that he degraded a year, or that he did not commence residence at the proper time.

He was elected Librarian on 24 March, 167¾, and was admitted the same day. Two years later, 23 Feb. 167⅞, the

---

[1] The name is found both as Manfeild and Manfield. The former is that in which he signs his name on his admission as Librarian, and it is that given in the School Register.

[2] Gardiner, p. 52.

work began of digging the foundations for the present Library[1]. Mr Manfeild was a subscriber of £20 to the fund for the erection and fitting up of the Library. He only held the office of Librarian till 1679, when (May 3) he was appointed Chaplain in the place of Mr Scattergood, and Mr Laughton succeeded him as Librarian.

From 1684 to 1686, Mr Manfeild was University Librarian. I owe to Professor Mayor a statement of the voting at his election,

> Manfeild, James, M.A.—116,
> Broughton, Thomas, M.A., Jesus College—78,
> Shorting, M., M.A., Jesus College—?

He appears as Chaplain in the Senior Bursar's books till 1686, in which he receives one quarter's stipend: he must therefore have ceased to be Chaplain at the end of 1685, or the beginning of 1686. How the Chaplaincy and University Librarianship were vacated, whether by death or otherwise, I am quite unaware.

In the *Threni Cantabrigienses* (Cantab., 1669) are verses by Jas. Mansfield (Trin.); and in the *Musarum Cantabrigiensium Threnodia* (Cantab., 1670), by Jas. Manfield (Trin.).

(VII.) JOHN LAUGHTON. [1679—168⅔.]

In the person of John Laughton, we come to one who was well known amid the literary men of his day, as we shall seek to show. For some of the details as to his family and birthplace, I am indebted to the kindness of my friend, the Rev. L. Borissow, Precentor of Trinity College, who has received them from Miss E. J. Laughton, of the Hollies, Tickhill, Yorkshire, the descendant of John Laughton's elder brother William. John Laughton was the younger son of John Laughton, gentleman, of Eastfield, Tickhill, and was baptized there 17 Jan., 1649[2].

[1] Conclusion of 22 February: Willis-Clark, ii. 537.

[2] It is suggested in the notes put in my hands, that, though in some family papers it is stated that John Laughton "dyed a batchelor," he may more probably be identified with the Rev. John Laughton, rector of Goadby-Marwood, Leicestershire, who married Dorothy, sixth daughter of Anthony Tate, Esq., of Burleigh Park. The College statutes, however, would prevent

He was entered, as pensioner, at Trinity College, under Mr Bainbrig, 1 May, 1665; and admitted Scholar 17 April, 1668. He took his degrees in due course, B.A. in $166\frac{7}{8}$, and M.A. in 1672. He was appointed Chaplain in 1678 and Librarian in 1679. I find no trace in the Conclusion-Book of his election to the Librarianship, but he was admitted 13 May, 1679. After a short time, however, he vacated his new office and went back to his old one, for on 17 Feb. $168\frac{4}{5}$, we find the Seniority appointing Mr Thomas Rotheram Librarian, and Mr Laughton Chaplain in the place of the said Mr Rotheram. On 22 Jan. 1686, Laughton was elected University Librarian[1], and held that post and his College Chaplaincy till his death in 1712. He also held prebends both of Lichfield and Worcester. He was collated to the former, 28 July[2], 1696, and to the latter, 22 May[3], 1700.

Laughton was an intimate friend of Sir Isaac Newton. This is shewn, for example, by two letters to Conduitt, Newton's nephew, from Humphrey Newton, who was Sir Isaac's amanuensis at Trinity, 1683—9. In one of these, dated 17 Jan. $172\frac{6}{7}$, he mentions that Sir Isaac rarely went visiting, and had but few visitors. Of these but three are named, of whom Laughton is one[4].

In a subsequent letter, 14 Feb. $172\frac{7}{8}$, he remarks: "Mr Laughton, who was then Library Keeper of Trin. Coll., resorted much to [Sir Isaac's] chambers: if he commenced Dr afterwards, I know not[5]."

Laughton from marrying, whether as Librarian or Chaplain. William Laughton died in 1702, aged 60, and is buried in Tickhill Church, where there is a monument to him. For a very full genealogy of the Laughton family, reference may be made to Hunter's *South Yorkshire*, vol. i. p. 246.

[1] Letters of Laughton at this period of his life, 1687—9, to Dr Charlett, Master of University College, Oxford, are in the Ballard collection in the Bodleian, xxiii. 1—13.

[2] Le Neve-Hardy, i. 612. The vacancy on Laughton's death was filled 2 March, $171\frac{1}{2}$.

[3] Le Neve-Hardy, iii. 83. The vacancy here on Laughton's death was not filled till 8 Nov. 1714.

[4] Brewster's *Memoirs of Sir Isaac Newton*, ii. 92, ed. 1855.

[5] *Ibid.* p. 96. Laughton did not proceed beyond the degree of M.A.

He was also on intimate terms with Newton's friend, Charles Montague, afterwards the first Earl of Halifax, who in a letter announcing to Newton his appointment as Master of the Mint (19 March, 169$\frac{5}{6}$) says, " Pray give my humble services to John Lawton (sic). I am sorry I have not been able to assist him hitherto, but I hope he will be provided for ere long, and tell him that the session is near ending, and I expect to have his company when I am able to enjoy it[1]."

Laughton was a man of great literary activity, and his name is frequently met with in the notices of scholars of his time. He was eminent as a book-collector, and his collection, or, at any rate, the choicer portion of it, was bequeathed to the College Library[2].

Of Laughton's own literary work we may notice, first, that he often appears as a writer in the University tributes of congratulation or condolence. He was the author of verses in *Hymenaeus Cantabrigiensis* (Cantab. 1683), *Maestissimae ac Laetissimae Academiae Cantabrigiensis Affectus* (Cantab. 168$\frac{4}{5}$), *Illustrissimi Principis Ducis Cornubiae...Genethliacon* (Cantab. 1688), *Musae Cantabrigienses* (Cantab. 1689), *Lacrymae Cantabrigienses in Obitum Serenissimae Reginae Mariae* (Cantab. 169$\frac{4}{5}$).

Besides these lighter effusions, he produced something more solid as the editor of the beautifully printed quarto edition of Virgil (1701; several times reprinted in octavo, 1702, 1707, 1711). According to Hearne, he wrote the " very long" Preface to the Cambridge edition (1687) of *Vincentius Lirinensis*[3]. He supplied the list of the MSS. in Trinity College Library to the *Catal. Librorum MSS. Angl. et Hib.* (1697). He corrected for Tho. Smith a transcript of Camden's *Annals of James*[4]. He helped Will. Piers in his edition of the *Medea* and *Phœnissœ*

---

[1] Brewster's *Memoirs of Sir Isaac Newton*, ii. 191.

[2] A detailed account of the early English part of this bequest will be found in my *Catalogue of English books printed before* 1601 *now in the Library of Trinity College, Cambridge.*

[3] Hearne's *Diary*, 4 May, 1707: vol. ii. p. 11, ed. Oxf. Hist. Soc. The preface is repeated in the edition of 1689, but in neither is there any mention of Laughton's name.

[4] Smith's pref. to *Camdeni Epist.*, London, 1691. 4to.

of Euripides, and Piers gratefully speaks of "humanissimus bibliothecæ publ. præfectus...amice et benevole, ut semper solet."

There seems a general consensus among writers as to the kindness and courtesy of Laughton as well as to his learning. Grabe tells us how Laughton ("vir erga exteros supra modum humanus") shewed him the Cambridge MS. of the *Testaments of the xii. Patriarchs*[1], and would have allowed him to copy it had he so wished[2].

Professor Mayor, to a note of whose[3] I owe most of the above instances, also cites Moses du Soul (Solanus) as speaking, in a note on Lucian[4], of an emendation, " quam [restitutionem] ante annos viginti a me repertam, non meis tantum libris adscripseram, sed in codice viri doctiss. Joh. Laughton, bibliothecæ Cantabrigiensis præfecti, amicitiæ causa."

The Strype correspondence in the University Library shews how much aid Strype received from Laughton. In a letter of Laughton's to Will. Gouge (7 Dec. 1689) Laughton tells of his search in Trinity Hall Library and elsewhere for a MS. life of Abp Parker[5], and refers to materials for the Elizabethan bishops generally. In 1697—8, he sends materials for Strype's life of Sir Thomas Smith[6].

In like manner, the references to Laughton in the *Diaries* of Burman and of Uffenbach on their visits to Cambridge, are couched in highly complimentary language. Burman reached Cambridge, 17 July, 1702, and, on the following day, "the very learned public Librarian, Laughton, escorted" him to see St John's College, and its Library. On the following day, Laughton shewed him Trinity Library and afterwards his own

---

[1] Fl. i. 24.

[2] Preface to *Test. xii. Patr.* in *Spicilegium*, vol. i. p. 336, ed. 1. Grabe ultimately printed the text of the *Testaments* from a transcript of the Cambridge MS. given him by John Mill, unfortunately of the most inaccurate character.

[3] *Cambridge under Queen Anne*, p. 328.

[4] *Demosth. Encom.* 33 fin.

[5] *Strype Correspondence*, vol. ii. 21 (*Cat. of MSS. in Lib. of Univ. of Camb.* v. 33).

[6] *Ibid.* 7, 8, 11, 14, 15 (*Cat.* v. 31, 32).

"very curious library and coins. He is...a man of great erudition; he has very lately edited Virgil[1]."

Uffenbach's visit took place in the Long Vacation of 1710, at a time when Laughton was unfortunately absent. This was a great disappointment to Uffenbach, for he complains, with reference to his visit to the University Library (1 Aug.), that of the MSS. "we could see nothing well, because the librarian, Dr[2] Laughton (or as they pronounce it, Laffton) was absent; which vexed me not a little, as Dr Ferrari highly extolled his great learning and courtesy. *Rara avis in his terris[3]*." Again, under date 13 August, he laments not having seen various learned and famous men, who were absent from Cambridge during the summer:—"Among them it is only fair to name first Dr Laughton, the *bibliothecarium* of the university. For if he had been in residence, we should (thanks to his singular courtesy, which was very highly commended to us[4]) not only have examined the public library more thoroughly and better, but also his own collections in *manuscriptis* and *nummis[5]*."

Besides his duties as Librarian, Laughton was a member of the first body of Curators of the Press ever appointed (Grace of 21 Jan. 169⅚). After the mention of the Vice-Chancellor, the Heads and Professors, comes, "Mr Laughton Coll. Trin. Academiæ Architypographus." I do not understand the exact force of the title[6].

Laughton's political opinions are sufficiently shewn by the fact that he was appointed to preach the sermon at St Mary's

---

[1] Mayor, *op. cit.* pp. 116, 117. Both Burman and Uffenbach very naturally speak of Laughton as Dr. This, however, is an error; he never proceeded beyond M.A.

[2] See preceding note.

[3] Mayor, p. 140. See also p. 153.

[4] In curious contrast to this is the letter (3 Aug. 1708) from Librarian Hudson to Hearne:—"...Call'd upon John Laughton. He did not so much as invite me either to eat or drink with him; wᶜʰ he might have done wᵗʰ out being in danger of my accepting his offerr: neither could he be prevail'd with to take a single copy of Livy. Leaving this poor mortal...." (In Hearne's *Diary*, vol. ii. p. 123; ed. Oxf. Hist. Soc.)

[5] Mayor, p. 194.

[6] Wordsworth, *Scholæ Academicæ*, p. 385.

before the University on 14 Feb. 168⅞, which was kept as a day of thanksgiving for deliverance from Popery and arbitrary power[1]. A brother Librarian, of a very different tone of thought, honest Tom Hearne, evidently held him, on political grounds, in high aversion. Thus in his *Diary* for 8 Oct. 1705, Hearne remarks, "M[r] Laughton (John) Keeper of y[e] Publick Library in Cambridge I am inform'd is a rank whig, a great Talker, and very violent in his Aspersions of the true Ch. of England Men[2]." It is perhaps worth noting that Laughton was a subscriber for Hearne's *Leland*[3].

Laughton's death is noted by Rud in his *Diary*, edited by Dr Luard for the Cambridge Antiquarian Society. Under the date 4 Sept. 1712, we read[4], "M[r] Laughton dyed about 6 this morning, at his niece Jenkins's house at Woodlayes near Rotheram." Hearne too thus records it under 18 Sept., "M[r] John Laughton, Keeper of the Publick Library in Cambridge, died lately. He was a learned man, and understood Books well, and left behind him a good collection, not only of Books, but old coyns etc.[5]" Hearne again refers to Laughton's books in a letter to Mrs Barnes, 29 Oct. 1712, "I have not yet heard how M[r] Laughton's books have went. But I do not doubt but they have been sold at great Prices, his collection (so far as I can gather) being extraordinary[6]."

Laughton's literary papers were bought at his death by George Paul. In a letter of 21 Aug. 1713 to Strype, then preparing his life of Whitgift, he remarks, "I have bought the late Mr Laughton's MSS. and papers of all kinds, and am pretty confident that there are many things amongst 'em w[ch] might be useful to you in your design'd Life of Abp Whitgift[7]."

[1] Alderman Newton's *Diary*, p. 98, ed. cit.; Cooper's *Annals*, iv. 2.

[2] Vol. i. p. 53. The editor's note on this passage (p. 354) in contrasting Hearne's verdict with Uffenbach's, speaks of Dr J. Laughton. As I have already said (p. 23, n. 1), Laughton did not proceed beyond M.A. Moreover, Hearne does not dispute Laughton's learning.

[3] Hearne's *Diary*, vol. iii. p. 81.

[4] p. 8.

[5] *Diary*, vol. iii. p. 458.

[6] *Ibid.* p. 477.

[7] *Strype Correspondence*, vol. iv. 85 (*Cat.* vol. v. p. 94).

These are referred to in a letter of Thomas Baker to Strype[1], 15 Aug. 1713. Shortly after this, Mr Paul died, as we learn from a subsequent letter of Baker to Strype[2]. Baker had bought the whole collection of Laughton's papers, yet does not seem sure of his legal title. He asks Strype, if he have any of his papers, to retain them till his title is clear.

The following is the inscription on a memorial tablet on the wall of Tickhill Church, "Jane Farmary Widow and Relict of Robert Farmary, Gent., gave a Plate to the Parish Church of Tickhill, for the perpetual use of the communicants there, in memory of her late dear brother, Rev. John Laughton, B.D.[3] of Trinity College, Cambridge, Keeper of the University Library, who departed this life, Sept. 4, 1712. Son of John Laughton, of Eastfield, Gent.[4]"

Laughton's arms were, quarterly, per fess indented, or and gules[5].

One regrets that this eminent Scholar has not found a place, surely amid many men of lesser note, in the *Dictionary of National Biography*.

(VIII.) THOMAS ROTHERHAM. [168⅔—169⅖.]

Thomas Rotherham or Rotheram (for both spellings occur even in his epitaph), was the son of Christopher Rotherham, "armiger," and Barbara his wife, and grandson of Sir John Rotheram, knight, of Someresse (Someries), in the parish of Luton, Bedfordshire.

It would thus seem clear that Thomas Rotherham was descended from John Rotherham, brother of Thomas Rotherham, Archbishop of York (1480—1500), to whom Cambridge owes so much; for the estate of Someries, which had belonged to the Wenlock family, was, on the death of Lord Wenlock, who was killed at the battle of Tewkesbury in 1472, forfeited to the

---

[1] *Baker Papers*, part ii. no. 73 (*Cat.* vol. v. p. 134).
[2] *Ibid.* no. 75.
[3] See p. 23, n. 1.
[4] Communicated by Miss E. J. Laughton.
[5] Hunter, *l.c.*

Crown, and was by the Archbishop procured from Edward IV. for his brother[1]. There the family of Rotherham abode for two centuries, till it passed by marriage into the hands of the Crawley family. Mr Guest, whose work I have cited, gives[2] a pedigree of the Rotherham family from the father of the Archbishop, but I cannot find the name of Christopher Rotherham occurring therein.

Christopher Rotherham had settled in London as a mercer; and after his death, his son was sent to St Paul's School, where he was an exhibitioner, 1652—1662, and received a grant of £5 on election to the Exhibition[3].

He was entered pensioner at Trinity College, under Mr Duport, 24 March, 165⅞, "Londinensis, e Schola Paulina," the school not being often noted in the Admission-Book at this early date.

He was not a scholar of the College[4]. He took the degrees of B.A. in 165⅞, and M.A. in 1660. On 9 April, 1661, he was elected to a supernumerary Chaplaincy. The Conclusion of that day runs that it was agreed that Mr Thomas Rotherham " be chosen conduct of this Colledge to come into the next place that shal be voide for him." A vacancy evidently occurred soon, for in the Senior Bursar's book for the year ending Michaelmas, 1661, Mr Rotherham receives one quarter's stipend, the other three quarters going to Mr Yates, whom he replaced. He retained the office of Chaplain for more than twenty years, and then vacated it in favour of Mr Laughton, himself becoming Librarian. He was elected Librarian 17 Feb. 168⅞, and admitted 8 March. The Conclusion Book under the former date records, "Ordered then by the Master and Seniors that Mr Thomas Rotherham be and is chosen Library-Keeper, and that Mr John Laughton be chosen conduct in the place of the said

[1] Guest, *Historical Notices of Rotherham*, p. 165. Mr Guest subjoins descriptions of the house at Someries as seen by Camden and Gough. See also, with some difference of detail, Lysons, *Magna Britannia*, i. 108.

[2] *op. cit.* p. 99.

[3] Gardiner, *Admission Register of St Paul's School*, p. 46.

[4] We have here a clear breach of Sir Edward Stanhope's order that the Librarian was to be "one that is or hath been scholler of the College."

Mr Rotheram. Jo. North, M^r. Coll." A record of the fact also occurs in the general Admission Book (sub ann. 1682), which is of so unusual a type in that book, being indeed the only one of the kind I have noted, that I transcribe it at length :—" Thomas Rotherham, Artium Mag. fil. Christophori Rotherham Armig., fil. Johannis Rotheram Equit. Aur. de Someresse in com. Bedford, a Magist. et Sen. Coll. SS. et Individ. Trinitatis a Sacellano electus Bibliothecarius ejusd. Coll. Feb. 15, 1682, et admissus Mar. 8."

On 6 April, 1665, a Thomas Rotheram, who must be the above, was incorporated as M.A. at Oxford, from Trinity College, Cambridge[1]. Mr Foster (l. c.) adds, "perhaps Rector of Pett, Sussex in 1695." As Librarian, Rotherham would have been incapable of holding a living, which was expressly forbidden by Sir Edward Stanhope's will, under pain of forfeiture ; but he became Chaplain again by exchange with Mr Banks in January, 169⅜, when such a plurality would have been possible. A subsequent Librarian, Samuel Doody, held a Chaplaincy and College living together in the last years of his life.

In the last year of Mr Rotherham's Librarianship, the books were moved into the present Library, and in the Junior Bursar's accounts for the year ending Michaelmas, 1695, we find the sum of £3. 6s. 0d. paid to the Porters for transferring them[2]. In the following year, when Mr Rotherham had become Chaplain, we have a Conclusion of 24 July, 1696, "Agreed then by the Master and Seniors that ten pounds be given to Mr Rotheram for his trouble in removing the Books out of the old Library into the new." Mr Rotherham had been a subscriber of £20 to the fund for the erection and fitting up of the Library.

Mr Rotherham died 8 Nov. 1702, in the sixty-sixth year of his age, and was buried in the ante-Chapel, on the east of the entrance. On the tomb-stone are Rotherham's arms :—Vert, three bucks trippant, or. Crest, a buck's head erased. Below this, is the following epitaph, "Thomas filius Christophori Rotherham Armigeri filij Johannis Rotheram equitis de Someries

---

[1] Foster, *Alumni Oxon.* sub nom.
[2] Willis-Clark, ii. 546.

in parochia de Luton in comitatu Bedfordiæ Art. Mag. & hujus Collegij Sacellanus dignissimus obijt Nov. 8 Anno {Dni. 1702 | ætatis suæ 66."

On the following Nov. 20, Mr Gale is chosen Chaplain in place of Mr Rotheram, deceased.

Le Neve, *Monumenta Anglicana*, iv. 48.
Blomefield, *Collect. Cantab.* p. 111, ed. 1750.

(IX.) JAMES BANKS. [169$\frac{5}{6}$—1706.]

James Banks (Bankes, Bancks) was entered as pensioner of the College under Mr Boteler, 10 Sept. 1678. He did not become a scholar[1]. He took the degrees of B.A. in 168$\frac{2}{3}$ and of M.A. in 1686. He was chosen "supernumerary conduct," 18 Dec. 1689, appearing as actual Chaplain in the Senior Bursar's book for the year ending Michaelmas, 1690, for which year he divides the stipend with Mr Devereux. He vacated the Chaplaincy and became Librarian, 14 Jan. 169$\frac{5}{6}$. A Conclusion of that day runs, "Agreed also by the Vice-Master and Seniors that Mr Thomas Rotheram be conduct in the place of Mr James Banks, and that the said Mr Banks be our Library keeper in the place of Mr Rotheram, they both consenting to this exchange. William Linnet, Vice-Master." Yet though this exchange took place in Jan. 169$\frac{5}{6}$, still in the Senior Bursar's book for the year ending Michaelmas, 1696, Rotheram receives the full payment as Librarian, and Banks in the following year.

On 3 July, 1700, a James le Bancks was incorporated M.A. at Oxford from Trinity College, Cambridge[2], who must be the one now before us, as there was no other James Banks of Trinity at that time.

On 19 Nov. 1706, James Banks, M.A., was instituted Rector of Lilley, Herts. (then in the diocese of Lincoln), on the presentation of Launcelot Docwra, Esq., of Putteridge, on the death of John Stone[3]. This living he resigned, and was succeeded by

[1] See p. 26, n. 4.
[2] Foster's *Alumni Oxon.* sub nom.
[3] Clutterbuck's *Herts.* iii. 88.

Thomas Cheyne, 13 Nov. 1709. Of course the acceptance of the living involved the cession of the Librarianship.

On 5 March, 1712, James Bancks was instituted Rector of Bury, Lancashire, on the presentation of "Thomas Bancks, by virtue of a donative from William, Earl of Derby, dated 12 June, 1676." Mr Banks held this living till his death, his successor, John Stanley, being instituted 19 July, 1743[1]. My friend and former pupil, the Rev. B. O. F. Heywood, M.A., of Trinity College, now Curate of Bury, informs me that he knows of no memorial of any kind of Mr Banks in Bury Church.

Mr Banks's shield is on the wall of the College Chapel, the easternmost on the South side. The arms are, Sable, a cross or, between four fleurs de lys argent. The tinctures must be considered doubtful. My friend the Rev. A. H. F. Boughey points out that with the same coat there are variations in tincture of the charges in different branches of the Banks family, and it is not possible to say with certainty to which of these the shield in the Chapel is to be referred.

(X.) Nicholas Clagett. [1706—1716.]

The spelling of the name of this Librarian varies between Clagett, Claget, Claggett and Clegat. The spelling of the surname here adopted is that in which he writes it when sworn in as Librarian. For the Christian name, I have taken the ordinary spelling, but Clagett in his will spells it Nicolas.

His father and grandfather both bore the same name as himself. His grandfather was in 1636 Vicar of Melbourne, Derbyshire[2], and died as preacher of St Mary's, Bury St Edmund's, 12 Sept. 1663. His son, Nicholas Clagett the second, was also preacher at St Mary's, Rector of Hitcham, Suffolk, Rector of Thurlow Parva, Norfolk, and Archdeacon of Sudbury. He died 27 Jan. 172$\frac{4}{5}$, at the age of 73. Archdeacon Clagett's brother, Dr Will. Clagett, was preacher at Gray's Inn, and died 28 March, 1688.

---

[1] Baines's *Lancashire*, ii. 517, ed. Harland.
[2] Foster, *Alumni Oxon.* sub nom.

Nicholas Clagett the third was educated at Bury St Edmund's School under Mr Leeds, and was entered as sizar at Trinity College, under Mr Laughton (formerly Librarian of the College, and at this time Librarian of the University and Chaplain of the College) on 14 April, 1702. During the years 1704, 1705, he acted as Under Librarian[1]. He was admitted scholar 28 April, 1704; and took the degrees of B.A. 170$\frac{5}{6}$, M.A. 1709, D.D. 1724.

As we have said, Mr Banks's acceptance of a living vacated the Librarianship, and three days after, carefully observing Sir Edward Stanhope's prohibition of delay, the Seniority proceeded to a fresh election. Under 22 Nov. 1706, there is a Conclusion, "Sir Clegat, Batchelor of Arts and Scholar of this College, was elected Library Keeper, in the room of Mr Banks, who vacated his place by accepting a living. Ri. Bentley, Mag^r Coll." Clagett retained his post till 1716, but what led to his resignation then I am unable to say. While he was Librarian, he acted on several occasions as "Tutor," as Laughton certainly, and Griffith as I believe, had done before him, though this was not strictly speaking in accordance with Sir Edward Stanhope's requirements. On 19 June, 1708, Thomas Trevor, eldest son of Lord Trevor, was admitted as Fellow-Commoner, under Mr Clagett; on 25 April, 1709, Thomas Sharpe, son of the Archbishop of York, was so admitted, as Pensioner; and on 1 Jan. 171$\frac{3}{4}$, William Belasyse, son of Sir Henry Belasyse, of Brancepeth, was so admitted as Fellow-Commoner (from Christ's College).

In a letter of Bentley to Archbishop Wake, of 13 Aug. 1728, while denying that his nephew, in his Librarianship, had ever accepted any office or lecture in the College, and so broken Sir Edward Stanhope's rule, he adds "but his Predecessors have frequently." He then cites the first two of the above[2].

Clagett was Librarian when Uffenbach paid his visit to Cambridge in 1710, on which occasion he examined Trinity

---

[1] Senior Bursar's books for those years, in Library account.
[2] *Bentley Correspondence*, p. 681.

Library on July 29, 30, Aug. 4[1]. Uffenbach mentions that it was his custom to confine his attention in the first instance to what a librarian regarded as most remarkable, "but afterwards I search for myself, having often found far better for myself, owing to the ignorance of many librarians which one cannot but wonder at and deplore[2]." He then proceeds to mention what Clagett showed him on this occasion. Certainly he made a curious choice to begin with, a transcript on vellum of the *Codex Bezæ* made for Archbishop Whitgift [B. 10. 3]. This was followed by "some oriental MSS.," a missal on vellum, a volume of "very fine sketches taken in Italy," and a "few coins in two drawers." Uffenbach makes no personal comment on Clagett, as he does on good Thomas Baker at St John's. A few years later, an English traveller speaks cordially enough. Ralph Thoresby, on his second visit to Cambridge, records in his *Diary* under the date 7 July, 1714, " He [Dr Colbatch] very courteously showed me the stately library, of which the obliging M[r] Claget is Keeper, whose company also I enjoyed[3]."

Like his predecessor Laughton, we find Clagett aiding Strype in his historical work. He catalogued for him the MSS. in Trinity Library containing the proceedings against Barret and Baro in 1595–6[4]. This now stands as B. 14. 9[5].

I have already said that Clagett resigned the Librarianship in 1716, though I do not know from what cause. About this time, however, he was Chaplain to Charles, Earl of Sunderland[6], and he may have received some appointment from him, or have been in attendance on his patron. Anyhow, in the autumn of 1717, he was made Rector of Pulham St Mary in Norfolk (his

---

[1] Professor Mayor's translation in his *Cambridge under Queen Anne*, pp. 126, 131, 153.

[2] *Ibid.* p. 126.

[3] vol. ii. p. 232, ed. Hunter.

[4] Cooper's *Athenæ Cantab.* i. 224 : ii. 274, 551.

[5] See *Strype Papers*, vol. vii. 39. *Cat. of MSS. in Lib. of Univ. of Camb.* vol. v. 90.

[6] Blomefield-Parkin, *History of the County of Norfolk*, iii. 266.

predecessor died 13 Oct. 1717) and retained it till 1721[1], when he was succeeded by Michael Clagett, M.A., doubtless a kinsman[2].

On 5 Oct. 1721, Clagett was presented by the Earl of Sunderland to the Rectory of Brington, Northamptonshire. He appears to have held this living till he became Bishop of *Exeter*, for his successor, Will. Mayo, M.A., who had been his curate, was not appointed till 30 Sept. 1742[3].

Clagett was appointed Archdeacon of Buckingham, 1 Sept. 1722[4]. Nichols mentions[5] a curious incident of this part of his life. While Clagett was at Hanover in 1723 with George I., the king gave him the Rectory of St Martin's in the Fields, and Clagett "actually kissed hands upon the occasion." The Lord Chancellor, however, had already presented Zachary Pearse to it, and on the king's return to England, the Chancellor carried the day.

It may have been by way of consolation for this that Clagett received his next preferment. He was appointed Dean of Rochester, 8 Feb. 172$\frac{3}{4}$[6]. He next became Bishop of St David's, in succession to Bishop Sydall; the date of the congé d'élire being 17 Dec. 1731, and that of the consecration, 23 Jan. 173$\frac{1}{2}$[7].

At this period of his life, Clagett was a friend of Browne Willis, the Antiquary, who in his will, dated 15 Dec. 1741, bequeathed "coins of five guineas value" to the Bishop of St David's and others[8]; but in a subsequent codicil he revoked all these bequests[9]. Willis survived the Bishop several years and died in 1760.

From St David's, Clagett was translated to Exeter in succession to Bishop Weston, and the appointment was confirmed

[1] Blomefield-Parkin, *l.c.*

[2] Presumably, Michael Clagett, Fellow of Queens' College, Cambridge; B.A. 170$\frac{4}{5}$, M.A. 1713.

[3] Baker, *Hist. and Ant. of the County of Northampton*, vol. i. p. 92 *b.*

[4] Le Neve-Hardy, ii. 71.

[5] *Lit. Anecd.* iii. 108 n.

[6] Le Neve-Hardy, ii. 578.

[7] *Ibid.* i. 304.

[8] Nichols, *Lit. Anecd.* viii. 220.　　　　　　[9] *Ibid.* 223.

in Bow Church, 2 Aug. 1742[1]. For the details of Clagett's Exeter life, save in so far as I refer to Le Neve, I am indebted to the kindness of Winslow Jones, Esq., of Exmouth, to whom also are due the accompanying references. Mr Jones further mentions, though not as a certainly established fact, that Clagett is said to have been collated by the Bishop (Willis) of Winchester, to the Rectory of Overton, Hampshire, 31 Oct. 1731.

On 2 Aug. 1742, the day on which Clagett was confirmed as Bishop of Exeter, he was instituted, *in commendam*, to the Treasurership of Exeter Cathedral, vacant by the death of Bishop Weston, on the presentation of George II.[2], and was also appointed Archdeacon and Prebendary of Exeter[3]. On 19 Aug. 1742, he was installed and enthroned[4], and on 21 Aug. he was elected Canon Residentiary[5], but he does not seem to have attended a single meeting of the Chapter.

He died 8 Dec. 1746, and was buried on 11 Dec. at St Margaret's, Westminster. He retained until his death the Bishopric, Treasurership, Archdeaconry, Prebend and Canonry, as well as the Rectory of Shobrooke. Dr George Lavington succeeded to all his preferments.

This grim picture of the abuses which were tolerated in the Church at the time is not even ended by death, for the note subjoined as to Bishop Clagett's will, which Mr Winslow Jones has kindly sent me, shows that for a year after death the Canonry was still in the grasp of the dead hand.

The will is dated 2 May, 1746, and a codicil 13 June, 1746, and was proved in the Prerogative Court of Canterbury, 16 Dec. following, by Samuel Clagett, the brother, and his friend Mr Daniel Gill, the executors.

By his will Bishop Clagett desired to be buried in the church or churchyard of the parish in which he should die, and the burial to be ordered in the most frugal manner. All his

[1] Le Neve-Hardy, i. 382.
[2] Archbishop Potter's *Register*, 279 *b*.
[3] *Ibid.* 280, 280 *b*: Le Neve-Hardy, i. 396, 429.
[4] *Dean and Chapter Act Book for* 1739....... p. 190.
[5] *Ibid.* 195.

personal estate is to be divided into three equal parts, and distributed between his brother Mr Samuel Clagett of St Edmund's Bury, and his sisters Mrs Jane and Mrs Margaret Clagett. To his nephew Mr William Clagett he gave £1 and no more, and to his nephew's mother one shilling, and he desired his brother Mr Samuel Clagett and his friend Mr Gill to undertake the execution of his will. By the codicil, he directed his *annus post mortem* in right of his Canonry of Exeter, to be divided into three parts between his brother Samuel and his sisters Jane and Margaret.

The following list of sermons published by Clagett is partly taken from Nichols[1], but the first two of those which he gives are shewn by the dates to be by Nicholas Clagett the father.

1. The Duties and Obligations arising from the Advantages of Life. A Sermon [on Luke xii. 48] preached at Bishop's Stortford in Hertfordshire, Aug. 31, 1714, at the Anniversary Solemnity of the School-Feast. By Nicolas Clagett, M.A., Library-Keeper of Trinity College in Cambridge...
1714 [Trin. Coll., Brit. Mus.]

2. A Sermon on the Consecration of White [Kennett], Bishop of Peterborough 1718

3. A Sermon [on 1 Thess. v. 12, 13] preached at the Consecration of Samuel [Bradford], Bishop of Carlisle, on Whitsunday, 1718 ....
1718 [Trin. Coll., Brit. Mus.]

4. A Spital Sermon, Easter Tuesday, 1720.............................1720

5. Sermon concerning Edifying; preached at All Saints Church in Northampton, Aug. 11, 1726, at the Triennial Visitation of the Rt. Rev. Father in God, White, Lord Bishop of Peterborough. By Nicholas Clagett, D.D., Dean of Rochester, Rector of Brington, and Chaplain in Ordinary to his Majesty'..1726

6. The recompense of God's faithful stewards. A Sermon [on Matt. xxv. 23] preach'd before the............Governors of the several hospitals of the City of London ....1729 [Brit. Mus.]

7. A Sermon [on 1 Cor. x. 24] preach'd............on Monday in Easter Week, March 26, 1733, being one of the Anniversary Spittal-Sermons ......
1733 [Brit. Mus.]

8. A Sermon [on 1 Tim. ii. 1, 2].........before the House of Lords......
Jan. 30, 1735, being the day appointed to be kept as the day of the martyrdom of King Charles the First ....1736 [Brit. Mus.]

---

[1] *Lit. Anecd.* i. 338.

9. A Sermon [on Acts xi. 18] preached before the Society for the Propagation of the Gospel in Foreign Parts, Feb. 18, 1736 ....
1737 [Trin. Coll., Brit. Mus.]

10. A Sermon [on Heb. xiii. 16] preached.........May 3, 1739, at the yearly meeting of the children educated in the Charity schools in London and Westminster. To which is annexed an account of the origin and designs of the Society for Promoting Christian Knowledge 1739 [Brit. Mus.]
Second edition ....1740 [Brit. Mus.]

11. A Sermon [on Ps. xcii. 1] preach'd...at Westminster, on the 11th June.........being the anniversary of His Majesty's......Accession to the Throne, etc. ....1742 [Brit. Mus.]

To these may be added

Articles of Enquiry upon which the Ministers, Church-wardens and Side-men of every parish within the Archdeaconry of Buckingham are to ground their presentments at the Visitation of the Archdeaconry of Buckingham, etc...1732 [Brit. Mus.]

Clagett had verses in the *Epicedium Cantabrigiense* (Cantab. 1708) on the death of Prince George of Denmark, the husband of Queen Anne.

The life of Archdeacon Clagett in the *Biographia Britannica* was written from "Memoirs" supplied by his son, the Bishop.

The Bishop of Exeter kindly tells me that there is no portrait of Bishop Clagett in the Palace at Exeter, and that none is known to exist in or about Exeter. I have also to thank the Bishop of St David's, who informs me that he possesses a pencil sketch of Bishop Clagett, taken from a painting, the present habitat which, however, he unfortunately forgets.

In the *Dictionary of National Biography*, it is remarked of Clagett[1], "he was doubtless educated at the grammar school in his native town, and proceeded thence to Cambridge, but again no particulars remain." One would have thought the *Graduati Cantabrigienses* a sufficiently familiar book, a reference to which would have given Clagett's College and degrees, when the College books might be trusted to give further details, as we have seen above.

---

[1] Vol. x. p. 366 *b*.

(XI.) WILLIAM CHICHELEY. [29 Sept. 1716—12 Jan. 171$\frac{6}{7}$.]

Clagett had resigned his post as Librarian at some time in the summer of 1716, though I am quite unaware as to the cause. The Master and Seniors, however, permitted the post to remain vacant longer than the fourteen days allowed by Sir Edward Stanhope to elapse between the knowledge of a vacancy coming to the College and the election of a new Librarian; and the Archbishop of Canterbury (Wake) accordingly availed himself of the power bestowed upon him by the will of the founder to appoint to the vacant post a person qualified under the conditions laid down in the will.

In the famous dispute between Bentley and Archbishop Wake in 1728, Bentley refers to the earlier incident of 1716, and states[1] that the post vacated by Clagett had been allowed to remain vacant in excess of the permitted time, in order that it might be bestowed upon the best of the Scholars who failed to obtain a Fellowship.

The Archbishop's nominee was William Chicheley[2] (or Chichley). He was the third son of Admiral Sir John Chichley, M.P., who was ninth in descent from William Chichley, Sheriff of London in 1410, the youngest brother of Archbishop Chichele, the founder of All Souls' College, Oxford[3].

William Chicheley was educated at Westminster, then under Dr Knipe, where he was admitted in 1705[4]. He was entered as pensioner at Trinity, 28 June, 1709, under Mr Baker, being then of the age of eighteen. In the Admission-Book, he is described as the son of the late John Chicheley, eques auratus of "Wimple" (Wimpole), Cambridgeshire.

He was admitted Scholar of the College, 22 April, 1710; and took the degrees of B.A. 171$\frac{3}{4}$, and M.A. 1716.

He was appointed Librarian by the Archbishop's mandate,

---

[1] *Bentley Correspondence*, p. 680.

[2] I spell the name thus at the head of the section because it is in this way that Chicheley spells his name at his Admission to the Librarianship.

[3] *Alumni West.* pp. 251, 252.

[4] *Ibid.* p. 245.

10 Sept. 1716, and was admitted on Sept. 29. In his declaration at Admission there is no reference to the action of the Archbishop, as we shall see in the subsequent case of Hutchinson. The fact is thus noted in Edward Rud's *Diary*, under the date 28 Sept. 1716, "They chose 5 Fellows...but were over-reach'd by Mr Chichely as to the Library-Keeper's place. It had laps'd to the Archbishop, and Mr C. brought down his Grace's mandate. D^r As[henhurst] did not like the man, and thereupon insisted mightily upon rejecting the mandate; which D^r B[entley] seem'd inclinable to do, till he was disswaded by a wiser head, and so he was admitted [1]."

Chicheley resigned the Librarianship after three months' tenure. He died *sine prole* in 1737.

Cole's MSS. xlv. 235, 334. *Alumni Westmon.* 245, 251, 252. In this latter, reference is made to documents in the possession of C. H. Chichley Plowden, Esq.

(XII.) EDWARD PEACH. [12 Jan. 171⅚—2 Oct. 1717.]

The new Librarian, like his predecessor, retained his office, it will be seen, for a few months only.

He was the son of Thomas Peach, of London, and had been educated at St Paul's School, then under Mr Postlethwaite. He was entered pensioner at Trinity, 11 April, 1710 (his father being then dead), under Mr Cotes. He was admitted Scholar, 14 April, 1711, and took the degrees of B.A. in 171¾ and M.A. in 1717 [2].

He was elected Librarian, on Chicheley's resignation, on 12 Jan. 171⅚, and was admitted on Jan. 25. On 2 Oct. 1717, he was elected and admitted Chaplain, thus vacating the Librarianship, and retained his Chaplaincy till 1737 inclusive [3].

On 1 Oct. 1737, John Baker, D.D., was elected Chaplain, and in the Senior Bursar's book for 1738, his name takes Peach's place. How the vacancy had arisen, I do not know.

---

[1] *Diary*, p. 18, edited by Dr Luard for the Cambridge Antiquarian Society.

[2] This last degree is wrongly omitted in the printed edition of the *Graduati.*

[3] His name occurs as Chaplain in the Senior Bursar's books from 1718 till 1737 inclusive, and then disappears.

In Mr Foster's *Alumni Oxonienses*, occur the names of John and Henry Peach, sons of Edward Peach, clerk, of Whitchurch, Oxon., both of whom matriculated at St John's College, Oxford, in 1757. Canon Slatter, the Rector of Whitchurch, kindly informs me that Edward Peach was never Rector of Whitchurch, but that a curate of that name was there in 1737. He can only trace one occurrence of the signature (viz. in 1737), but from the identity of the handwriting of the entries in the Register, he is disposed to think that the entries from 1727 to 1748 are in Peach's writing.

The name of Edward Peach does not occur in the list of members of the University of Oxford given by Mr Foster, nor is any to be found in those of Cambridge, save our present Librarian. The following fact given me by Canon Slatter makes it reasonably probable that the curate of Whitchurch had previously been the Librarian of Trinity. In 1723, Samuel Walker became Rector of Whitchurch, and retained his post till 1768. He had been a Fellow of Trinity College, Cambridge, and had taken his B.A. in 171$\frac{2}{3}$, M.A. 1716. He was therefore one year senior in College standing to Peach, and they were scholars of the College at the same time. Consequently, Walker may have been glad to give to an old College friend the curacy of his living, which was evidently a sole charge, from the continuous appearance of one handwriting in the Register, which is not Walker's, for twenty-one years.

(XIII.) Samuel Doody. [1717—1721.]

Samuel Doody was the son of Joseph Doody, of Stafford, and was educated at the Charterhouse, under Dr Walker. At the age of 17, he was entered as pensioner at Trinity, 30 June 1711, under Mr Pilgrim. He was admitted Scholar, 1 May, 1713, and took the degrees of B.A. 171$\frac{4}{1}$ and of M.A. 1718. On 3 July, 1722, he was incorporated as M.A. at Oxford, as Samuel Darby[1].

I do not find any reference in the Conclusion Book to his

---

[1] Foster's *Alumni Oxon.*, sub nom.

election as Librarian, but he was admitted, 2 Oct. 1717. He held his post for four years to the day, for his successor was admitted 2 Oct. 1721. Doody became Chaplain on ceasing to be Librarian, though again I find no record of his election or of his admission. However, the date of Bentley's admission as Librarian shews when the change was made; and Doody clearly became Chaplain at the beginning of the academic year 1721–22, for in the Senior Bursar's book for the year ending Michaelmas, 1722, Doody receives the full year's stipend as Chaplain.

On 19 Dec. 1721, he was presented by the College to the Vicarage of Monks' Kirby, in Warwickshire, holding the living and the chaplaincy together. He died in the autumn of 1727 (I do not know the date more exactly), and on Oct. 28 the vacant chaplaincy was given to Mr Smith, and on 29 Jan. 172$\frac{7}{8}$ the Vicarage was given to Mr Joseph Key, Master of Arts of the College. The date of Mr Doody's death might perhaps have been recovered from the Monks' Kirby Register, but I learn through the kindness of the Rev. W. E. Jackson, the present Vicar, that the Registers are missing for the years 1717—1733 inclusive.

A posthumous gleam of Mr Doody meets us in the Junior Bursar's book for the year ending Michaelmas, 1729, where among payments received is one "from Mr Doody's Executor, £10, for the plate lost by the said Mr Doody."

(XIV.) Thomas Bentley. [1721—1729.]

After one or two holders of the office, as to whom it is difficult to do more than collect a few unimportant facts, we come, in the person of the new Librarian, to a scholar who himself stood high in the world of letters, and is still better known from his connection with his famous uncle, Dr Richard Bentley, Master of Trinity, the "awful Aristarch" of the *Dunciad.*

Thomas Bentley was the son of James Bentley, the elder brother of Richard Bentley, of Oulton near Wakefield, gentleman. He was educated at St Paul's School, then under Mr

Postlethwaite; and was entered, at the age of sixteen, as pensioner at Trinity, under Dr Syke (Sike), on 19 Dec. 1707. We have in the Appendix to Dr Luard's edition of Edward Rud's *Diary*, a letter, dated 20 Nov. 1707, from Dr Bentley to Mr Postlethwaite respecting his nephew. Thomas Bentley, when staying in Trinity, had "given such a specimen of his studiousness and discretion," that his uncle had already been pressed by several to admit him to the College. This Dr Bentley would not do without communicating with Mr Postlethwaite, but since the nephew is now sixteen years of age and would be capable of taking Holy Orders by the time he commenced M.A.[1], the uncle proposes to admit him at Christmas and desires Mr Postlethwaite to send him to Cambridge as soon as the holidays begin[2]. Another letter follows from Dr Bentley to Dr Stubbe, the Vice-Master, dated 27 Jan. 1708, when Thomas Bentley was in his first term of residence, in which he remarks, "I ...... particularly am glad that my nephew deserves your good opinion[3]."

Thomas Bentley was admitted Scholar, 13 May, 1709, and Minor Fellow 2 Oct. 1714, becoming Major Fellow 8 July, 1715. He took the degrees of B.A. 171½, M.A. 1715, and LL.D. 1724.

The younger Bentley was evidently an amiable man, of scholarly tastes, and apparently of somewhat delicate health. Thus in a letter of Jeremiah Markland to Mr Bowyer (22 Nov. 1764), it is remarked, "Dr Bentley used often to say to his nephew, *Tom, I shall thrash thee*, meaning that he should outlive him[4]." The uncle was thirty years older than the nephew, and survived him by six weeks.

The earliest literary work of Thomas Bentley appeared in 1713, while he was still merely a B.A. It was a small edition of Horace [Q. Horatius Flaccus, ad nuperam Ricardi Bentleii editionem accurate expressus. Notas addidit Thomas Bentleius

---

[1] As a matter of fact, Thomas Bentley did not take Holy Orders, and thus his Fellowship would have lapsed.

[2] *Op. cit.* p. 41.

[3] *Ibid.* p. 42.

[4] Nichols, *Lit. Anecd.* iv. 331. See also *Bentley Correspondence*, p. 660.

A.B. Coll. S. Trinitatis apud Cantabrigienses alumnus. Cantab. typis Academicis, impensis C. Crownfield, 1713], in which he reproduced his uncle's text, with the various readings in the margin, and with notes of a somewhat elementary character. As Bishop Monk remarks[1], doubtless the large size and high price of Dr Bentley's *Horace* had led to a rather small circulation, and probably the uncle was glad to give his text a wider publicity through the agency of his nephew's "small" edition. Moreover, it was not an unnatural thing, that Dr Bentley having dedicated his *Horace* to the Earl of Oxford, Thomas Bentley should dedicate his to Lord Oxford's son, Lord Harley. He states that his uncle suggested the plan of the book, but had not seen it before its publication.

Attacks were made upon this work from two very different quarters. In 1717, Richard Johnson, Headmaster of Nottingham School, put forth a work, whose full title may be cited as a specimen of the good old style :—" Aristarchus Anti-Bentleianus, Quadraginta Sex Bentleii Errores super Q. Horatii Flacci Odarum Libro Primo Spissos Nonnullos, Et Erubescendos : Item per Notas Universas in Latinitate Lapsus fœdissimos Nonaginta Ostendens." In the Preface to this work it is suggested that the work bearing the nephew's name is in reality that of the uncle, who took the opportunity of applauding himself[2]. It is obvious that the charge is absurd and improbable in the highest degree.

The next attack, which takes a different stand, came from a very different quarter, Pope's *Dunciad*. In the first edition of this poem (1728) a couplet ran

> "* * his mouth with *Classic* flatt'ry opes,
> And the puft *Orator* bursts out in tropes[3]."

In the edition of 1729, Welsted's name was inserted in the place of the asterisks. In 1736, "Welsted" was replaced by

---

[1] *Life of Richard Bentley*, Vol. i. p. 340, ed. 2.
[2] "Cùm sub fratris filii nomine libri compendium fecerit, in quo præter inverecunda cætera, se Seculi Decus ipse appellat." *Præf.* p. viii.
[3] Book ii. ll. 187, 188.

"Bentley[1]." In this last edition, Pope gives the following malignant note on the passage :—

"Not spoken of the famous Dr Bentley, but of one Tho. Bentley, a small critic, who aped his uncle in a little Horace. The great one was intended to be dedicated to the Lord Halifax, but (on a change of the ministry) was given to the Earl of Oxford; for which reason the little one was dedicated to his son the Lord Harley. A taste of his *Classic Elocution* may be seen in his following panegyric on the Peace of Utrecht. ...But that this gentleman can write in a different style, may be seen in a letter he printed to Mr Pope[2]."

What the letter is which is referred to in the last sentence does not appear. Presumably Thomas Bentley, who seems to have been warmly attached to his uncle, had written a letter, not now traceable, in the public journals. Mr Courthope[3] thinks that "probably the letter was written in consequence of Pope's notes signed 'Bentley' to the 'Sober Advice from Horace,' which was published in 1734, and called forth a protest from Richard Bentley the younger." Dr Monk[4] conjectured "from circumstances" that the letter was written in 1740, but Mr Courthope points out that the note itself appeared in the edition of the *Dunciad* of 1736.

In 1718, Thomas Bentley brought out at Cambridge an edition of Cicero's *de Finibus*.

It will be remembered that, in Dr Bentley's letter to Mr Postlethwaite, he referred to the possibility of his nephew taking Holy Orders. The younger Bentley, however did not so proceed, and consequently under the then Statutes, his Fellowship would lapse after the expiration of seven years from his

---

[1] Pope's *Works*, vol. iv. p. 283, ed. Elwin and Courthope. The reading is there cited of what is called the "first Broglio MS.," in which "Bentley" stands in l. 187.

[2] *Ed. cit.* p. 145.

[3] *Ibid.* p. 331.

[4] *Op. cit.* vol. ii. p. 464. Here Dr Monk cites a letter from Pope to Warburton, who had suggested to the poet "some ludicrous comparison, as applicable to the uncle and nephew." He replies, "Your simile of B——— and his nephew, would make an excellent epigram. But all satire is become so ineffectual, when the last step that virtue can stand upon, *shame*, is taken away...." Whatever Bentley's faults were, one can but feel indignant at this Thersites-like malignity.

M.A. degree. Some months before the limit was reached, Mr Doody resigned the Librarianship, as I have already said, and on 2 Oct. 1721, Bentley was admitted Librarian, but I find no entry as to his election in the Conclusion-Book.

In Knight's *Life of Dr John Colet* [1724], Thomas Bentley's name occurs in the list of subscribers. It will be remembered that he had been a Pauline.

In 1725 and 1726, we find Thomas Bentley collating MSS. for his uncle, and doing other learned work, at Paris, Lyons, Rome and Naples. Seven letters from the nephew to the uncle are printed in the *Bentley Correspondence*[1], and describe the work and movements of the former. The first of the seven is written from Paris, and being imperfect the date is lost, but the others range in date from 16 Nov. 1725 to 2 Aug. 1726, during the whole of which time Thomas Bentley was on the Continent. As these letters are in print, it is sufficient here to say that they testify alike to very considerable learning on the part of Thomas Bentley, and to affectionate relations between nephew and uncle. At Paris, the traveller met, among other scholars, Montfaucon, Banduri and Harduin. There is a remark in the first letter from Rome, evidently referring to the Old Pretender; —" I have seen him. He has not $\epsilon\tilde{\iota}\delta o\varsigma\ \check{a}\xi\iota o\nu\ \tau\nu\rho a\nu\nu\iota\delta o\varsigma$[2]." In a later letter, he has just seen the famous Vatican MS. (Cod. B.)—" The Gr. Test. that Mico did for you. That's a Glorious Old Book. I have a good mind to collate it again for curiosity[3]."

There is no direct reference in these letters to the Library of which Thomas Bentley was Librarian. Once, when speaking of Mark Antony's Aqueduct at Lyons, he says " in one place where it crosses a valley, 'tis as high as our Library[4]." Again, he asks leave to purchase books at Rome, " that would be very fit for a Library," and suggests some, adding, " It will look like doing something as Library Keeper[5]."

With the year 1728 came the curious and intricate dispute between Richard Bentley and Archbishop Wake as to the

---

[1] Pp. 627 sqq.　　　[2] P. 636.　　　[3] P. 656.
[4] P. 646.　　　[5] P. 660.

Librarianship. The story is fully told in Bishop Monk's *Life of Bentley*, and as it is a matter appertaining to the history of the elder Bentley, rather than to that of his nephew, I shall only briefly indicate the course of the dispute. There is, in the Archiepiscopal Library at Lambeth, a large mass of papers [no. 1156], through which I have carefully worked, but nearly all of special interest have been printed in the *Bentley Correspondence*. I have already embodied in the section on Clutterbuck the documents in connection with him, and some others will be cited in a note appended to this and a following section.

On 28 June, 1728, Colbatch, alike one of the ablest as he was one of the most persevering of Bentley's adversaries, together with Parne petitioned the Archbishop to intervene in the matter of the Librarianship, which they declared Thomas Bentley had forfeited, both by his long absences from his post, inasmuch as during six or seven years he had never been in residence for more than three months in any one year, and also because he had taken the degree of LL.D. in defiance, it was said, of Sir Edward Stanhope's regulation. The petitioners then recommend to the Archbishop, Sandys Hutchinson, B.A. and scholar of the College, for the post.

The Archbishop having communicated with the Master, the latter replies, and his letter is given in the *Bentley Correspondence*[1]. As regards the first of the two charges, what I have already said as to Thomas Bentley's Continental travels will show that there was a good deal of laxity in the matter, and the uncle does not dispute the fact, but defends it by saying that his nephew had worked at Greek and Latin MSS. in various Continental Libraries, with the view to publication; that this was done at his own expense, and that he had appointed a Deputy Librarian. As regards the other charge it will suffice to say that it is clear that Sir Edward Stanhope's meaning was that no one should be appointed Librarian, who, at the time of appointment, was of over M.A. standing. This is at once shown by the fact that in the case of a Librarian proceeding to a higher degree after his appointment, no penalty is provided by

[1] P. 680.

Sir Edward, which he is very careful to do in other cases. Bentley goes also into other points, *e.g.* his nephew had not taken any other office, though his predecessors had frequently done so; Clagett is named as an example. He shows further that various orders had become obsolete, and that the College had itself very considerably increased the value of the post, and *pro tanto* had a right to have a co-ordinate voice with the Founder's Will. The land bought with the Stanhope bequest brings in, says Bentley, £32 per annum, but the present charges to the College of Librarian and Under-Librarian were £77.

A vigorous correspondence ensued, in which Richard Bentley's letters are characterised by a marked ingenuity and by a system of truly Fabian tactics. Though doubtless Thomas Bentley can have had no special desire to retain a post at which he was hardly ever present, yet an argument was drawn up in his name, and this is subscribed by the Master and eight Fellows, to the effect that they are satisfied with his reasons and that the post is not vacant. Bishop Monk justly observes[1] that the style of the document, professedly the work of the nephew, is unmistakeably from the pen of the uncle. Indeed the last paragraph, which Bishop Monk cites, can only be called contemptuous.

After a time, the Archbishop, probably getting weary of the matter, proposed to Bentley (10 Dec. 1728) to leave the decision to the Attorney-General (Sir Philip Yorke), and he, on 1 March, 172⅞, declared that Thomas Bentley had not forfeited his post under the conditions of Sir Edward Stanhope's will, and that, as he had not received three admonitions for neglect from the Master and Seniors, the post was not vacant. This would have made an end of the matter, had it not been that the Archbishop had already nominated as Librarian Sandys Hutchinson, who had been recommended by Colbatch and Parne, and he was disposed to stand upon his assumed rights. One would have thought that, if the Attorney-General were right, as one cannot doubt, there never had been a vacancy, and therefore

---

[1] Vol. ii. p. 277.

the Archbishop had no *locus standi*. At this stage, Thomas Bentley resigned the Librarianship, and on 20 June, 1729, a successor was appointed. The Conclusion runs " Agreed by the Master and Seniors that Mr Gossipp be chosen into the place of Library Keeper, now void by the voluntary cession of Dr Thomas Bentley. Ri : Bentley."

The further story of the dispute has now no connection with Thomas Bentley, but must be spoken of in connection with Gossip and Hutchinson.

A note of Mr Bowyer refers to Thomas Bentley under the year 1730. In that year, the oration before the University on Jan. 30, in memory of Charles I., was delivered by John Taylor, M.A., Fellow of St John's, afterwards Librarian and Registrary of the University. On this Nichols[1] cites a MS. note of Mr Bowyer ;—" Thomas Bentley, an awkward imitator of his uncle Richard, attacked the Latinity of this Oration, criticising anonymously in a newspaper the first sentence, as an unusual construction without two infinitive moods after *fore*; which the Doctor vindicated in conversation, by authorities both ancient and modern. He was abused in the same channel for saying the Scots sold their king; a fact well attested." Bowyer does not give his authority for his statement.

Some years later, in 1733, an accident befell Thomas Bentley, the effects of which were disastrous, and might well have proved fatal. He had had entrusted to him by Dr Mead the unfinished notes of Dr John Davies on the Philosophical writings of Cicero. These he was to edit, and to continue the notes on the *de Officiis* from the point where Davies had left it unfinished at his death. Accordingly Thomas Bentley devoted himself to this work at his lodgings in the Strand, but having contracted the dangerous habit of reading in bed, he managed to set the house on fire, and had barely time to escape with his life. All his papers were destroyed, including the whole of Davies's notes, and some unedited *scholia* on Homer[2]. Bishop

---

[1] *Lit. Anecd.* iv. 491 n.

[2] Monk ii. 357. See the authorities there cited, especially the life of Davies in the *Biographia Britannica* (vol. iii. p. 1618 n.).

Monk mentions to condemn an unfounded view which attributes the fire not to Thomas Bentley, but to his uncle.

Thomas Bentley brought out two works in the concluding years of his life. In 1741, appeared his edition of the *Hymns* of Callimachus, Theognis, etc., with Latin translation and notes[1]: and in 1742 an edition of Cæsar, with Dr Jurin's notes and emendations added. This work must have been published not long before Thomas Bentley's death. He was in ill health and was sent to Clifton for change of air. One day he went for an excursion on the river, was taken very ill, and died before he could be landed. He is buried in the church at Clifton, with the following inscription: Hic jacet corpus | Thomæ Bentley LL.D. | Qui obiit xxviii Maii | Anno 1742, | Ætat. 50[2]. His famous uncle survived him a little more than six weeks.

NOTE A.

Among the documents of the Wake-Bentley controversy in the Lambeth Library, are some papers connected with John Kay, under-Librarian in 1728, which show that besides the main dispute, of which I have already spoken, and of whose future outcome I must speak in the two following sections, there was also another curious side play. It is true that these papers have no bearing on the life of any actual Librarian, but as (to the best of my knowledge) nothing has ever appeared in print on the matter, and as it throws further light on the troubled College history, I have thought it worth dwelling on here.

John Kay, the son of William Kay of Caythorpe, was educated at Kirk-Leatham School, under Mr Thomas Clark, and thus was a schoolfellow of Gossip and Hutchinson. On 1 July, 1723, being then 18 years of age, he was entered as sub-sizar at Trinity under Mr Walker, afterwards Vice-Master, cruelly immortalized by Pope.

---

[1] For some remarks as to the aim of this work, see Wordsworth, *Scholæ Academicæ*, p. 110.

[2] Monk ii. 408.

Kay was under-Librarian during the years 1724—30 inclusive, as is shown by the Senior Bursar's books. He never took a degree, a matter which is referred to in the affidavit subjoined, as well as in his letter to John Mawer, and elsewhere, yet on 12 March, 172$\frac{4}{5}$, he was presented by the Vice-Master (Baker) and Seniors to the Vicarage of Roxton, then vacant by the cession of Mr Penson.

He evidently belonged to the party of Bentley's sympathisers in the Collegé, and so may well have been brought before the Archbishop's notice by the leading members of that party, as against Hutchinson, who was backed by Colbatch and Parne, the Master's keenest foes.

The beginning of the story is told in the affidavit [Lambeth 1156, no. 29], and therefore, though the affidavit is itself of later date than some of the other documents, I give it first. It bears two embossed stamps for sixpence each. It runs as follows:

I, John Kay, under Library keeper of Trinity College in the University of Cambridge, make oath, that on Thursday, 3rd October (as I believe) about one of the clock in the afternoon, Dr Walker, one of the fellows of the said College, called me from the gate, which is called the Queen's gate, where I was with three or four other lads, and asked me if the Head Library Keeper's place should be resigned, whether I could like it better than the preferment I am now possessed of: I answered yes; and gave him my Reasons for it, which he said he approved of, and ordered me to wait upon Dr Baker, one of the Fellows and Vice-Master of the said College, and tell him so. Dr Walker likewise said that I must resign all that I now had and take my Degree before I could be qualified for the place. I afterwards (according to Dr Walker's directions) waited upon Dr Baker at his chambers and gave him an account how far I had proceeded in regulating the Catalogues of the Library, which he wished me to go on with. Because if the Head Library Keeper's place should become vacant, it might be some recommendation to the Bishop (*sic*). At the same time he told me that we wanted a Resident Head Library Keeper to keep it in order, and to prevent so many lads from coming into the Library: he also said he would let me know when I should wait upon the Master about it, because the Master liked to have every person speak for himself.

This is the sum of all that passed between Dr Walker, Dr Baker and me to the best of my remembrance relating to the said Library Keeper's place.

Dr Walker went out of town on Thursday the 3rd inst. immediately after he had spoke to me, as is above mentioned and is not yet returned to College, nor have I had any letter nor received any message from him since he left this place.

Neither did Dr Baker speak one word to me about this affair from the time above mentioned that I was with him at his chambers till Saturday the 19th of this instant and so came to me to desire me to recollect and write down all that had passed between me, Dr Walker and himself, concerning the Head Library Keeper's Place, which accordingly is now done.

JOHN KAY.

Jurat coram me viceno nono die Octobris 1728.

JAMES WHISKIN[1].

The next reference in point of time is in a letter [no. 10] of Parne to the Archbishop, dated 9 Oct. 1728, where it is remarked,

"To my certain knowledge y⁰ Place hath been offered to y⁰ under Librarian within these few days. Tho' as he had no degree, nor could have any til y⁰ Term began (which it doth tomorrow) and fearing y' Grace might nominate one who might contest it with him, He hath not yet accepted of it. Nor wil it do him any good, for he must quit other things of very much worth, to have it."

We next come to an undated letter of the Archbishop [no. 16], which, however, I should assign to about Oct. 14, to the Master, in which after expressing his surprise that he had not been informed of the result of the meeting of the Seniority he remarks,

"Instead of this, I had an account which I thought I might depend upon [this of course refers to Parne], that the place had been offered to another person, who though not at that time qualified for it, (as having no degree), yet, the term coming on, might soon obtain one; and so my right of nomination be defeated for want of being beforehand in asserting it."

He therefore sent the nomination by Saturday's post[2].

---

[1] James Whiskin was Mayor of Cambridge in 1717, on the occasion of George I.'s visit, and in 1728 on that of George II. (Cooper's *Annals of Cambridge*, iv. 150, 198.)

[2] *Bentley Correspondence*, p. 688. The Saturday would clearly be Oct. 12, for Bentley, writing to the Archbishop on Sunday, Oct. 20, says that he received the nomination from Mr Parne and Mr Hutchinson "last Wednesday

No. 21 of the Lambeth papers is, I think, the answer to the foregoing. It is a repudiation of the charge contained in the Archbishop's letter, on the part of the Master and Seniors. They declare that they had discussed the question on Oct. 1 and at several meetings since, and the delay was accounted for by the Librarian's illness. There was no desire to waste time so that the Archbishop's time for appointment might lapse. They ask who it was that had written to the Archbishop. This is dated Oct. 19, and is signed by the Master, and Drs Baker V.-M., Hacket, Craister and Paris, and Joh. Myers, B.D.

Closely following on this, we have Parne's letter to the Archbishop of Oct. 24 [no. 19]. In this Parne states that he has learnt that on the previous Monday (Oct. 21) a paper, intended to be laid before the Archbishop, was sent round to some persons to be signed in the name of the Master and Seniors, though only half the Seniors were in College, and the paper was not laid before the [next[1]] most senior. Parne does not know the contents of the document, as "it was managed so very privately." He has learnt, however, one thing, that the Archbishop is asked to tell the Master and Seniors who it was that informed him of the offer of the Librarianship to the Under-Librarian about the beginning of October. He asks the Archbishop, if he thinks proper, either to send his letter to the Master or to name him directly.

The Archbishop's answer to this is dated Oct. 25 [no. 20]. He begins by citing part of his (undated) letter to the Master, and part of the statement of the Master and Seniors to which I have already referred, which concluded with the words "nor was any offer made of the Library Keeper's place with our knowledge and privity." The Archbishop will not mention Parne's name, in spite of leave given, unless Parne "can effectually justify" his account against this declaration. Clearly in face of the mention of Dr Baker in Kay's affidavit, the declaration can

afternoon," i.e. Oct. 16, so that the letter of the Archbishop may well have been written on Monday, Oct. 14.

[1] This word in brackets is not in the original, but the sense clearly requires it.

only be justified by explaining it of the *corporate* action of the Seniority.

I would also refer to two letters of Mr Greaves, Commissary of the University and Registrar of Trinity College, to the Archbishop[1]. In the earlier of these [no. 25], dated 28 Oct.[2], 1728, from 7 King's Bench Walk, Temple, he mentions that he had told the Archbishop at their interview that he had received Kay's account in his own handwriting, which would have been sworn to before him, had not he left Cambridge for London on the previous Monday morning, before Kay had returned from his living. This certificate [no. 18], dated Oct. 22, he had sent to the Archbishop. The draught of the Archbishop's letter is written on the back of Mr Greaves's letter, and in a second letter from the latter [no. 27], dated Oct. 30, which explains the confusion as to the two certificates, he forwards the affidavit itself.

The only other letter I need mention is one from Kay to John Mawer[3] [no. 24], at that time a B.A. scholar of the College and a former schoolfellow of Kay. What we have at Lambeth, however, is evidently not the actual letter, but a very rough draught. The writing is absolutely distinct from that of nos. 18 and 29, and can only be called a scrawl. It is neither signed nor dated, but internal evidence connects it undoubtedly with Kay, and the date must of course be October, 1728, and before the interview with Dr Baker referred to in the affidavit. The piece of paper is very jagged and torn, and before being used for the draught of the letter, had evidently begun to be used for another purpose, for there is a reference to Guillim's Heraldry on the reverse side.

In this letter Kay asks for a little money, as he may have to take a degree. He mentions the complaint to the Archbishop

---

[1] See Monk's *Bentley*, ii. 272.

[2] Wrongly endorsed on the outside, Oct. 29.

[3] John Mawer was educated at Kirk-Leatham School under Mr Clark (for whom see note under William Gossip), was entered as pensioner at Trinity under Mr Smith, 20 June, 1721, and was admitted Scholar 6 April, 1722. He took the degrees of B.A. 172⅔, and M.A. 1736.

about the Librarianship, and adds that Dr Walker had asked him if he would like to be Head Library Keeper.

"You will not be at a loss for my answer, seeing you know how much I like a College life. So he referr'd me to Dr Baker for further information, for he was going to take horse on some journey; whom I have not yet discoursed with, for he was engaged when I waited on him. I hope our malcontents will get nothing by the troubles they give the M', but I may perchance be bettered by them and little to their satisfaction."

Kay then wishes Mawer to write an *epithalamium* for " Miss Jugg's[1]" marriage. They made " a very handsome appearance at Sturbridge[2]."

Of Kay's subsequent history I know nothing.

NOTE B.

The extract in the following is not indeed strictly relevant to the subject of this work, yet I have inserted it here as being the only allusion to the architectural character of the Old Library that I ever met with. It is taken from no. 7 of the Lambeth documents, which is the answer by Colbatch and Parne to Thomas Bentley's argument. Clearly, for some reason, Bentley and his party fancied it suited their interest to lay as much stress as possible on the immense change involved in the removal to the "new Library"; Colbatch and Parne on the other hand seek to minimise the difference.

The statement following is given as the second of two things which have been affirmed, " which, if they are anything to the purpose, are by no means true":—

"That the old Library was made out of Garrets, and wou'd only hold three or four thousand Books; and is now fitted into Garret Chambers again. Whereas it was built on purpose for a Library, and just such a Garret as a great part of the Bodleian Library is, that is a lofty Room with a vaulted and curiously wrought roof, though in the third story; and it would commodiously hold ten or twelve thousand books."

---

[1] This is Miss Joanna Bentley, who was married to Mr Denison Cumberland in the summer of 1728.

[2] Sturbridge Fair was "proclaimed" on Sep. 18. See Wall-Gunning, p. 129.

It continues,

"Great part of it on the Removal of the Books to the New Library was fitted up by the Duke of Somerset into Lodgings for his own Family, when any of them shou'd come here. Two of his Grace's sons successively kept in them ; nor is there any but our own, and one or two more M⁷ Lodges in Town which have so stately a set of apartments in them. A Fourth part indeed or more of it was seized by the Ma⁷ and let out, as if it had been a Garrett over part of his Lodge."

(XV.) WILLIAM GOSSIP. [1729.]

I have cited in the preceding section the Conclusion by which Gossip was elected Librarian by the Master and Seniors, in order to complete the story of Thomas Bentley's tenure.

William Gossip, "filius G. (presumably Gulielmi) Gossip, e comit. Ebor." was educated at Kirk-Leatham School in North Yorkshire, then under Mr Clark[1], and was entered as pensioner at Trinity, under Mr Robert Smith, afterwards Master, 17 June, 1722, being then 17 years of age.

He was admitted Scholar, 3 May, 1723, and took the degrees of B.A. 172⅚ and M.A. 1729. He was elected Librarian, as I have said, on 20 June, 1729, but I find no trace of his admission.

Clearly, if the Archbishop had been justified in his nomination of Hutchinson, the resignation of Thomas Bentley, and the subsequent election of Gossip, could not affect matters ; and the Court of King's Bench was applied to on behalf of Hutchinson to issue a mandamus to the College to admit the Archbishop's nominee.

The reception of the mandate on the part of the College is

[1] In the Admission Book it runs "sub præsidio Dⁿⁱ Clark," *Dominus* of course standing for B.A. This must have been a slip on Gossip's part, for Thomas Clark, who was Head-master of Wakefield Grammar School from 1703 to about Easter, 1720, and then became Head-master of Kirk-Leatham School, was M.A. when appointed to Wakefield. For an account of this very able Head-master see *The History of Wakefield Grammar School* by M. H. Peacock, M.A., the present Head-master. Mr Peacock informs me that many of Mr Clark's pupils followed him when he was transferred from Wakefield to Kirk-Leatham. Whether Gossip was one of these does not appear. A subsequent Head-master, the Rev. John Clark, Fellow of Trinity College, was one who did so.

shown by the following Conclusion of 25 September, 1729 :—
" Agreed by the Vice-Master [Baker] and Seniors, that whereas
a Mandamus hath been served upon the College from the Court
of King's Bench, for the Admission of a Library Keeper, nominated by His Grace the Arch-Bishop of Canterbury, by a Power
claimed by His Grace under Sir Edward Stanhope's Will,
Mr Sharp be forthwith wrote to, to take opinion of council (sic),
how the College ought to proceed."

In the interval of waiting comes the one trace which I can
find of Gossip's actually discharging the duties of Librarian.
A Conclusion of 23 Oct. 1729 orders :—" Agreed also that Mr
Gossip shall be appointed to take care that the several manuscripts, medals, great globes, and skeletons, belonging to the
College, be forthwith brought into the Library: and that he
revise the catalogue of the manuscripts; and that he make a
catalogue of the medals: and that for the future no person be
permitted to take any manuscript[1], medal, great globe or
skeleton, out of the College Library, without leave from the
Master and Seniors." Whether Counsel, when appealed to,
spoke discouragingly, or whether Bentley, in view of impending
contests, had had enough of the controversy, I cannot say.
Anyhow the decision arrived at is clearly due to Bentley's
ingenuity : Hutchinson is to be accepted as Librarian, simply
under the terms of the Founder's will; Gossip is to be additional Library Keeper, appointed by the College. It will be
remembered that Bentley had informed the Archbishop how
much the College had augmented the original Stanhope bequest.

Two Conclusions of 3 November, 1729, run as follows :—
" Agreed by the Vice-Master and Seniors, that Sandys Hutchinson, Batchelor of Arts of this college, be admitted Library
Keeper upon the terms and conditions of Sir Edward Stanhope's
last Will and Testament."

---

[1] As regards MSS. an order to this same effect had been put forth by the
Seniority on 15 April, 1673, during the mastership of Isaac Barrow. The
repetition of the order on the present occasion is suggestive of considerable
laxity of practice.

"Agreed by the Vice-Master and Seniors, that Mr Gossip, Master of Arts of the College, be appointed additional Library Keeper, and that the College will make him satisfaction for his trouble."

Yet it must be noted that spite of the promise to Gossip, I find no trace of his name as receiving payment "for his trouble" in either the Senior or the Junior Bursar's books. The only reference to him of any kind is in the Junior Bursar's book for the year ending Michaelmas, 1729, under " Extraordinaries":—"To Mr Gossip for searching ye Register at York concerning ye Endowment of the Vic. of Kirby Lonsdale... £00. 03. 04."

In 1729, there was a close contest for the Vice-Chancellorship between Dr Lambert of St John's (Tory) and Dr Mawson of Corpus (Whig), when the former received 84 votes as against the 83 of the latter. Mr Gossip voted for Dr Mawson[1].

(XVI.) SANDYS HUTCHINSON. [1729—1740.]

The Archbishop's nominee was the son of Edward Hutchinson, of Boston, Lincolnshire, gentleman, who had died before his son entered Trinity College. He was educated at Kirk-Leatham School, under Mr Clark, and probably was one of those who followed his schoolmaster thither from Wakefield. I have already mentioned that I have learnt from Mr Peacock, the present Head-master of Wakefield School, that a good many boys did so follow their master. That Hutchinson was one of these would seem to follow from the fact that he was a donor to the Wakefield School Library in 1729[2].

He was entered as pensioner at Trinity, on 23 June, 1724, under Dr Smith, afterwards Master, being then 18 years of age. He was admitted Scholar, 16 April, 1725, and took the degrees of B.A. in $172\frac{7}{8}$, and M.A. in 1731. He also incorporated as M.A. at Oxford on 22 July, 1732[3].

---

[1] Cole's MSS. xl. 31.   [2] Peacock, p. 169.
[3] Foster, *Alumni Oxon.* sub nom.

The manner in which he was connected with the dispute between Dr Bentley and the Archbishop has been already mentioned, the first occurrence of his name in the matter being, so far as I have observed, in the petition of Colbatch and Parne of 28 June, 1728 [Lambeth, 1156, no. 1 *bis*]. This seems to have been sent to the Archbishop, together with a letter of Sir Hardolph Wasteneys, the uncle of Hutchinson, dated Headon, 28 August, 1728 [Lambeth, no. 5 *b*], which is an answer to a letter of the Archbishop, which does not seem to be forthcoming.

Sir Hardolph urges the two main points on which Colbatch and Parne laid stress, and appeals to their petition in corroboration, and maintains that the Archbishop has power to fill up the place. He had clearly been shewn Bentley's letter of Aug. 13 to the Archbishop, after the receipt of which the Archbishop had evidently tried to quiet matters. Thus Sir Hardolph remarks, " Your Grace is pleased to take notice in the close of your letter that you have no authority in Trinity College[1]," and reminds him of his action in 1716, when Chicheley was appointed, and then presses the claims of his nephew " as a proper person for the place." At the end of the letter is the following postscript :—" I beg that your Grace will please to conceal the name of my Nephew, till y' Grace has determined the affair in his favour[2]."

The reply of the Archbishop to the above is not forthcoming, but, as appears from Sir Hardolph's second letter [no. 9], dated Headon, 21 Sept. 1728, it bore the date Sept. 12. The second letter, after going over old ground, asks for a Mandate to the Master and Seniors to confer the post on his nephew (still unnamed). There is a postscript to this letter also. Sir Hardolph states that his nephew is with him at Headon, and has just received a letter from one of the Fellows of Trinity, who tells him that if the Archbishop will be so good as to give him

---

[1] See also *Bentley Correspondence*, p. 684.

[2] It seems strange that Sir Hardolph should be thus urgent for privacy, seeing that Colbatch and Parne had openly declared the name of their candidate in their petition.

the Mandate, it must be under the archiepiscopal seal, and that the Master and Seniors must admit him in three days after receiving it. He therefore suggests that the Mandate be sent to Headon, and his nephew shall then return to Cambridge. "It is the opinion of his friends there that if he got your Grace's Mandate before the Seniors meet (which will be the latter end of this month), they will never dispute it."

The Archbishop, who surely must have been heartily sick of the affair, in a letter to Dr Bentley (undated, but clearly written about the middle of October), tells him that he had sent "a Nomination[1]." This is referred to by Dr Bentley in his letter to the Archbishop of Oct. 20[2],—" Your Grace's nomination was delivered to me by Mr Parne and Mr Hutchinson last Wednesday afternoon." The Archbishop himself was clearly not anxious to fight for his own nomination, for in his subsequent letter of Dec. 10[3], he expresses himself as quite willing to leave the whole matter to the judgement of the Attorney-General.

We have seen that legal steps were taken, though not apparently till the following autumn, to force the College to submit, and we have already shewn the final outcome which was reached, doubtless through Bentley's ingenuity.

On 3 Nov. 1729, the College accepted Hutchinson as Stanhope Librarian, and he was admitted on Nov. 11. The form used on that occasion is unusual, and was evidently worded in the light of the Conclusion of Nov. 3 :—" Sandys Hutchinson, juratus et admissus in Librarium super nominationem Reverendissimi in Christo Patris Archiepiscopi Cantuariensis secundum tenorem Testamenti Domini Edvardi Stanhope, Militis, hujusce Collegii aliquando Socii."

Thomas Bentley had resigned in June, 1729, yet in the Senior Bursar's book for the year ending Michaelmas, 1729, Bentley receives the whole year's stipend; in 1730 and following years Hutchinson's name appears alone, without Gossip's.

---

[1] *Bentley Correspondence*, p. 688.

[2] *Ibid.* p. 689.

[3] *Ibid.* p. 692.

Hutchinson was one of the four editors of Stephani *Thesaurus Linguæ Latinæ*, in four volumes folio; Cambridge, 1734. The other three were, the Rev. Edmund Law, M.A., Fellow of Christ's [afterwards Bishop of Carlisle], John Taylor, M.A., Fellow of St John's, and the Rev. Tho. Johnson, M.A., Fellow of Magdalene. At this time, at any rate, Hutchinson was not in Holy Orders[1].

It was during Hutchinson's Librarianship that the Library was robbed ´by Henry Justice. This unhappy man was a Fellow-Commoner of the College, and pleaded at his trial (March, 1736) that he was thereby a member of the Foundation, and as such could not be said to steal when he was himself part owner. Such a plea was of course quite inadmissible, and Justice was transported[2].

I do not know how Hutchinson's tenure of his office came to an end.

NOTE.

I give this note on a point of genealogy here, so as not to break the thread of the narrative. Although Sir Hardolph Wasteneys is so careful to abstain from mentioning the name, yet his nephew was of course Sandys Hutchinson, as is shewn by the simple fact that in the petition of Colbatch and Parne, which he forwards to the Archbishop, Sandys Hutchinson is definitely named.

In Burke's *Extinct and Dormant Baronetcies*, it is stated[3] that Sir Edward Wasteneys, the third baronet [ob. 1678], married Catherine Sandys, the great grand-daughter of Edwin Sandys, Archbishop of York. They had two children, a son, afterwards Sir Hardolph Wasteneys [ob. 1742], with whom the title became extinct, and a daughter, Catherine, who married Edward, the son of Samuel Hutchinson, of Boston, Lincolnshire.

---

[1] For remarks on this edition, see Nichols, *Lit. Anecd.* ii. 65, iv. 494, v. 176.

[2] For an account of the trial, see *Proceedings at Session of Peace and Oyer and Terminer for the City of London and County of Middlesex*, March, 1736; and for Justice's family, see Davies, *Memoir of the York Press*, p. 193.

[3] P. 555.

It is added that the only child of this marriage was a daughter and heiress.

It seems clear, however, that Sandys Hutchinson must also have been a child of this last marriage, for if Burke were correct, Sir Hardolph Wasteneys would not have had a nephew at all. Moreover, Sandys Hutchinson too was the son of an Edward Hutchinson of Boston, and his Christian name is the same as the maiden name of Catherine Hutchinson's (née Wasteneys) mother.

(XVII.) TIMOTHY LEE. [1740–1742.]

Timothy Lee[1] was the son of William Lee, of Pontefract, Yorkshire, and was educated at Westminster School under Dr Friend[2].

At the age of 18, he was entered at Trinity as pensioner, 6 Dec. 1732, under Dr Smith. He was admitted Scholar 20 April, 1733 ; and took the degrees of B.A. 1736, M.A. 1740, and D.D. 1752. He also incorporated M.A. at Oxford, 30 July, 1741[3].

He appears to have only narrowly missed a Fellowship. In a letter from Thomas Goodwin[4] to Samuel Jebb, both of Trinity College, it is remarked, "Yesterday came on the Election for fellowships, when there were seven Vacancies and nine Candidates : one of ye persons yt were thrown out was Leigh [this must be Timothy Lee], ye other you don't know." Goodwin then sends greeting from Mr Leigh, who "is just recovered of a

---

[1] An earlier Timothy Lee, born 18 Dec., 1659, possibly the grandfather of the above, was admitted at Merchant Taylors' School in 1673. (Robinson, p. 281.)

[2] The name does not occur in the *Alumni Westmonasterienses*, which seemed to me puzzling in the case of one who in due time became a Scholar of Trinity. Dr Rutherford, the Head Master of Westminster, kindly gives me the explanation :—"Apparently there was some reason why he should not be in College at Westminster. He may have been over age or under age, or delicate, or the like ; and at that time the Scholarships at Trinity and the Studentships at Christ Church were not open to town-boys."

[3] Foster, *Alumni Oxon.*, sub nom.

[4] Goodwin was afterwards Fellow ; B.A. 1742, M.A. 1744. Jebb did not proceed to a degree.

fit of sickness." Cambridge seems to have been visited by "a very malignant Distemper" in the preceding summer[1].

He was elected Librarian, 14 July, 1740, and admitted the same day. The cause which had led to the vacancy is not stated.

As will be seen, he vacated the Librarianship by accepting a living. He married Penelope, daughter of Sir William Chester, bart., and widow of John Price, of Covent Garden, surgeon. She was one of the co-heirs of Sir Henry Wood, to property in Suffolk[2].

Mr Lee became Vicar of Pontefract in 1742, Vicar of Felkirk, near Barnsley, in 1743, and Rector of Ackworth, near Ponte-fract, in 1744. He died at the age of 63, at Ackworth, 19 April, 1777, and was buried there, but no tombstone or tablet to him is known there. His wife had died at Ackworth, in 1762, of consumption and was buried there.

My cordial thanks are due to the Rev. J. H. Littlewood, Vicar of Felkirk, and the Rev. H. Howlett, Rector of Ackworth, for the information they have kindly given me. Mr Howlett has written for the "Ackworth Parochial Magazine" a series of papers on the "Antiquities of Ackworth," and has sent me copies of those which refer to Dr Lee and his relations to the parish. Parts of these, in a condensed form, I subjoin. Dr Lee was evidently a man of great energy, and varied parts. It is recorded of him that he kept a pack of hounds for the amuse-ment of his parishioners, and it is not at all improbable that he shared in the amusement himself. He employed an expert to make a transcript of all the Parish Registers, from the earliest date to his own time, and also to make fair copies of the ancient and half illegible deeds contained in the Parish Chest, relating to the charities and other matters of local interest.

He assisted in the consolidation of the various charities now grouped under the head of the "Poor's Estate." The greatest

[1] This letter, with others to the same, is given in Wordsworth's *Scholæ Academicæ*, p. 312.

[2] Gage, *Hist. and Ant. of Suffolk, Thingoe Hundred*, pp. 393, 399. See also *Notes and Queries*, 4th series, v. 549, vii. 304.

work, however, carried out under his auspices was the enclosure
of the parish by a private Act of Parliament, passed in the year
1774, by which definite portions of land were assigned to the
various freeholders, in lieu of the "Common Rights" hitherto
enjoyed by them. Dr Lee considerably improved the method
of keeping the Parish Registers, and in the case of Burials was
in the habit of recording the cause of death. In reference to
this, Mr Howlett calls attention to the terrible havoc wrought
in the parish a hundred and fifty years ago by small-pox, and
contrasts this with the comparatively rare presence of the
disease there of recent years.

During the Rectorship of Dr Lee, a Foundling Hospital was
established at Ackworth, on land bought in 1757 by the governors
of the London Foundling Hospital from Sir John Ramsden and
others. The intention was to found a branch institution, where
the weaker children might be benefited by country air, and where
there would also be increased facilities for apprenticing the children. For a time the children were lodged in a farm-house, but
ultimately extensive buildings were erected, which now form
the Friends' School. Dr Lee was one of the foremost and most
energetic members of the Hospital Committee and it was he
who designed the centre and principal building. The water
supply was planned and worked out by Smeaton, who built the
Eddystone Lighthouse. The total cost of the building was
£12,000, a much larger sum of course in those days than at
present. The Hospital remained at Ackworth from 1757 to
1773, when, owing to the withdrawal of a Parliamentary grant,
this and two other branches had to be given up. A work on
the history of the school, which took the place of the Hospital
(*The History of Ackworth School*, by Henry Thompson, of
Arnside), to which Mr Howlett acknowledges his obligations,
but which I have not succeeded in seeing, says of Dr Lee's
services to the Hospital:—"While speaking of the general
success of the Institution, it would be a mistake to omit
reference to Timothy Lee, D.D., to whom so much of that
success, if not absolutely due, was much indebted. He was a
gentleman who placed an intelligent and philanthropic mind

almost entirely at the service of the young institution; and living within sound of its clock bell, was ever able to be at the place, at important and critical moments, unstintingly lavishing time and love upon its welfare."

It is worth adding that a special caravan was constructed to carry the children and their nurses from London to Ackworth by the Great North Road, the journey occupying in fine weather six or seven days; and that "Dr Lee invented an ingenious kind of hammock, which was slung inside the caravan, in which the little ones could sleep at night."

Strong evidence of the esteem in which Dr Lee was held in his parish is furnished by the following statement, written on the back of his portrait, which now hangs in Ackworth Rectory :—

"Timothy Lee, S.T.P., was presented to the Rectory of Ackworth, December, 1744. He died there April 19, 1777, aged 63, universally lamented, as before he had been beloved and honoured by his Parishioners.

"This portrait, painted by the elder Kellingbeck, of Pontefract, a few years before Dr Lee's death, and esteemed to be a strong likeness, is presented by one of his successors to the Rector and Churchwardens of Ackworth for the time being, for the use of the Parish, in the hope that it may be allowed to remain in the Rectory House, as a mark of respect to the memory of the original."

Mr Howlett has most kindly had the portrait photographed for me. Dr Lee is represented in gown and bands, and the face is a most striking combination of geniality and shrewdness.

As far as appears, Dr Lee had no children of his own, but a mural tablet in Ackworth Church, to the memory of his step-daughter and her husband, contains the only reference to Dr Lee known to Mr Howlett in or about the Church. It seems strange that neither the step-daughter, who left a charity to the Parish, nor the parishioners, should have raised some monument to one so "universally lamented."

The tablet runs as follows :—"Sacred to the Memory of Anthony Surtees, Esq., one of His Majesty's Justices of the Peace for the West Riding of Yorkshire, and many years Lieut. Col. of the 2nd West York Regiment of Militia. He died 12th January, 1807, aged 65. Also of his wife Frances

Dorothea Surtees, who died 27th of March, 1802, aged 64. She was the daughter of Penelope, the wife of John Price, Esq., who afterwards married Timothy Lee, D.D. and Rector of this Parish."

(XVIII.) Thomas White. [1742-1763.]

Thomas White was the son of Richard White, of Wakefield, was educated at Wakefield School, under Mr [Benjamin] Wilson[1], and was entered as sub-sizar at Trinity, under Mr [John] Wilson, on 21 March, 173⅘, being then 19 years of age. He was a Storie Exhibitioner from Wakefield School in 1740[2].

He was admitted Scholar, 10 April, 1741; and took the degrees of B.A. 174½, and M.A. 1745. He was elected Librarian, 30 Dec. 1742, "on the cession of Mr Lee," and was admitted the same day.

He held the Librarianship till his death[3], 30 Aug. 1763. He had taken Holy Orders[4].

I have no details to mention as to Mr White's long tenure of office of twenty-one years. The only notice of him which I can find shews anyhow that it was not an inactive one. A Conclusion of 15 Dec. 1767 runs, "ordered by the Master and Seniors that the Senior Bursar pay the late Mr White's Executrix seventy pounds for six Folio Volumes, containing part of a new Catalogue of the Books in the College Library."

(XIX.) Thomas Green. [1763-1788.]

Thomas Green was the son of Thomas Green, of Wimeswould (Wymeswould), Leicestershire, and was educated at Loughborough School under Mr Parkinson.

At the age of 18, he was admitted as sizar at Trinity,

---

[1] Peacock, p. 135. Mr Benjamin Wilson was Head-master of Wakefield School, from 1720 to 1751. He had been a Fellow of Trinity: B.A. 171⅘, M.A. 1719. It has been thought by some that Goldsmith's portrait of Dr Primrose is drawn from the Rev. Benjamin Wilson (Peacock *l.c.*). Mr John Wilson was his younger brother.

[2] Peacock, p. 189.

[3] *Gentleman's Magazine*, vol. xxxiii. p. 465.

[4] *Ibid.*

11 June, 1756, under Mr Whisson[1]. He was admitted Scholar, 11 May, 1759, and took the degrees of B.A. 1760, and M.A. 1763. He was elected Librarian 12 Sept. 1763, and was admitted the same day. The Conclusion recording his election states that the post had become vacant through the death of Mr White.

He was elected Professor of Geology by the Senate, 7 May, 1778[2], and retained both the Librarianship and the Professorship till his death, which took place at Cambridge, 9 June, 1788[3], when he was fifty years of age. He had taken Holy Orders[4]. He was buried at St Michael's on June 11[5].

A contemporary account states that in the autumn before his death he had been deprived of the use of one side by a paralytic stroke, while shooting in Huntingdonshire; and he was with difficulty brought home to College. He was thence sent to Bath, but "found no relief from its waters." The writer adds, "His goodness of disposition and his botanical knowledge, made him regretted by all who knew him[6]."

With regard to his Professorship, it is stated in the *Cambridge Calendar* for 1820, in a notice, believed from the style to be Professor Sedgwick's, that Professor Green "added some valuable organic remains to the Woodwardian cabinets[7]."

(XX.) John Clark. [1788–1803.]

John Clark was the son of John Clark, of London, and was educated at Petersfield School, Hants., under Mr Street. He was entered at Trinity as sizar, 3 June, 1780, under Mr Collier[8], being then twenty years of age. He was admitted Scholar,

[1] See for Mr Whisson, Dr Luard's article in the *Trident*, p. 11.

[2] *Cambridge Chronicle* for 9 May, 1778.

[3] *Cambridge Chronicle* for 14 June, 1788.

[4] *Ibid.*; see also *Gent. Mag.* infra.

[5] Venn, *Register of St Michael's Parish*, p. 159, edited for the Camb. Ant. Soc.

[6] *Gentleman's Magazine*, vol. lviii., part 1, p. 565.

[7] P. 37, referred to in Clark-Hughes, *Life and Letters of Adam Sedgwick*, i. 194. It is there stated that Professor Green bequeathed books for the use of the Lecturer.

[8] Luard, *u. s.*, p. 14.

2 May, 1783. He took the degrees of B.A. (as 4th Senior Optime) in 1784, and M.A. in 1788. He was elected Librarian, 23 June, 1788, and was admitted the same day.

In one of Porson's letters to Hailstone, dated 23 Feb. 1790, he sends a jocular message to Mr Clark :—"Please to tell the Right Rev^d the librarian that I have got a copy of the new Edition of Toup's critical works, published at Oxford, which copy is at the library's service, if it chuses to accept it[1]." I suppose from this that Mr Clark was in Holy Orders, but I have no other evidence.

He held the Librarianship till his death, as is shewn by the Conclusion recording the appointment of his successor.

(XXI.) CHARLES HOYLE. [1803–1804.]

Charles Hoyle was the son of Robert Hoyle, of Halifax, and was educated at Hipperholme School, near Halifax, under Mr Hudson. At the age of sixteen he was entered at Trinity, 11 July, 1789, as pensioner, under Mr Jones[2]. He was admitted Scholar, 20 April, 1792; and took the degrees of B.A. 1794, and M.A. 1797. He won the Seatonian Prize in 1804 and 1806. He was elected Librarian, 31 May, 1803, and was admitted on August 16.

The biographer of the Rev. Legh Richmond, who had taken his degree from Trinity in the same year with Mr Hoyle, states that an early (unnamed) friend had reported that Mr Richmond's "first attempt to preach *ex tempore* in the very small church of Yaverland, in the Isle of Wight, was a total failure." Much ashamed, he declared that he would not try again, but did so on the "urgent solicitation of our common friend, the Rev. Charles Hoyle," and was most successful afterwards[3].

In 1812, Mr Hoyle was presented by the Duke of Marlborough, whose domestic Chaplain he was, to the Vicarage of

---

[1] *Correspondence of R. Porson*, p. 48 ; edited by Dr Luard for the Cambridge Antiquarian Society.

[2] Luard, *u.s.*, pp. 16, 118.

[3] Grimshaw, *Memoirs of the Rev. Legh Richmond*, p. 111, ed. 11.

Overton in Wiltshire, and retained it till his death. He died at Overton, and is buried in the churchyard there. The inscription on the head-stone runs, "In remembrance of the Revd Charles Hoyle, 36 years vicar of this parish, who died the 15th day of November, 1848, aged 76 years[1]."

Mr Hoyle published the following works:—

1. Moses viewing the Promised Land. Camb., 1804. [Seatonian Prize Poem.]

2. Paul and Barnabas at Lystra. Camb., 1806. [Seatonian Prize Poem.]

3. Exodus, an Epic Poem in Thirteen Books. London, 1807.

This is dedicated to the Duke of Marlborough, whose domestic Chaplain Mr Hoyle then was.

4. Three Days at Killarney, with other Poems[2]. London, 1828.

5. The Pilgrim of the Hebrides; a lay of the North Countrie. By the author of Three Days at Killarney[3]. London, 1830.

6. Exodus, or the Curse of Egypt, a Poem[4].

To these may be added,

7. A Sermon [on Matt. xvi. 18] preached at...Marlborough...at the Visitation of the...Bishop of Salisbury. Bristol, 1823 [Brit. Mus.].

In no. 4, the influence of Sir Walter Scott's *Lord of the Isles* and *Lady of the Lake* is very prominently marked.

(XXII.) ALDOUS EDWARD HENSHAW. [1804–1837.]

Aldous Edward Henshaw was the son of Edward Henshaw, of Cambridge, and was educated at Linton School, Cambs., under Mr Lodge. He was entered at Trinity, as sizar, under Mr Jones, 6 July, 1798, being then 17 years of age.

He was admitted Scholar, 22 April, 1803, and took the degrees of B.A. in 1804, and M.A. in 1807. He was elected Librarian 14 Dec., 1804, and admitted Dec. 16.

---

[1] Communicated by the Rev. F. W. Welburn, Vicar of Overton.

[2] This is published anonymously. I assign it to Mr Hoyle, on the authority of Halkett and Laing, col. 2584.

[3] *Ibid.* col. 1913.

[4] Whether this is a later edition of no. 3, or an independent poem, I do not know. I take it from the *London Catalogue of Books published in the years* 1816—1831.

He took Holy Orders, and was "for many years officiating minister at Bottisham, Cambs." He died 13 Dec., 1837, "at the South-sea-house," aged 56[1].

(XXIII.) CHARLES WARREN. [1837–1840.]

Charles Warren was the third son of the Rev. Dawson Warren, M.A. [of Trinity College, Oxford; Vicar of Edmonton, 1796–1838], and was born at Edmonton, 16 Sept., 1808. He was educated at Hammersmith school, under Mr Railton; and was entered at Trinity under Mr Peacock (afterwards Dean of Ely), 19 March, 1827.

He rowed "three" in the first inter-university boat race in 1829, when the late Dean Merivale was "four," and the late Bishop Selwyn "of Lichfield and New Zealand" was "seven."

He was admitted Scholar 23 April, 1830, and took the degrees of B.A. 1831, and M.A. 1834.

He was ordained deacon, 29 April, 1832, and priest 28 April, 1833, by Bishop Marsh of Peterborough. He became curate of Burton-Latimer, Northants. (29 April, 1832), of Edmonton (30 May, 1834), and Perpetual Curate of St James, Enfield Highway (16 July, 1835).

On 26 Dec., 1837, he was elected to the Librarianship, vacant through the death of Mr Henshaw, and was admitted the same day. He held this post until it was vacated by his acceptance of the Vicarage of Over, on the Western borders of Cambridgeshire. Of this the College had been the patron since its foundation, but, in 1839, the presentation had somehow been allowed to lapse. A Conclusion of 2 Dec. 1839 agrees that "Mr Warren, now Librarian to the College, be recommended to the Bishop of Ely, for his Lordship's License to the sequestration

---

[1] *Gentleman's Magazine*, New Series, vol. ix. p. 215. He was of course not Vicar, for he could not have held a living with the Librarianship, but Curate, perhaps in sole charge. The living could be held with a fellowship: Mr Pugh was Vicar 1810—26, and Mr John Brown (for whom see Luard, *u.s.* p. 107) from 1826—37. Mr Henshaw also officiated at St Michael's, Cambridge, as we see from Dr Venn's edition of the Parish Register.

of Over." The Bishop himself allowed the presentation to lapse
to the Crown, and it was by the Crown that Mr Warren was
actually presented.   He was instituted 3 Sept. 1840.   The
Librarianship, however, had been vacated some months before
this, for Mr James Ind Smith was elected on 12 March, 1840,
"in the room of Mr Warren, now Vicar of Over."   This last
phrase, I presume, means that the living had been offered and
accepted, though the formalities were delayed.

Mr Warren was in 1842 Proctor in Convocation for the
Diocese of Ely.   He resigned the living of Over in 1873, and
resided for the latter part of his life in Cornwall.   He died at
Kenwyn, 17 Dec. 1883.

Mr Warren was the author of

1. Sermon for Enfield National School, 1837.
2. Indeterminateness of Unauthorised Baptism, 1841.
3. The Lord's Table the Christian Altar, 1842.
4. Address to Parishioners of Over on opening the National School,
1843.
5. Sermons for Over National School, 1845.
6. Ministry of the Word for Absolution, 1849.
7. Letters on Sisterhoods in *Evening Journal*, 1852.
8. Five Sermons for the National Society, 1855.
9. Swainson on Article xxix.   Review in *Ecclesiastic*, Feb. 1857.
10. Discipline the Defence of Doctrine.   Three papers [the second
called "The Church at the Revolution"] in *Ecclesiastic*, June—
Aug. 1857.
11. Sermon in Ely Cathedral at the Second Diocesan Choral Festival,
1860.
12. Ely Substitute for Diocesan Synods, 1866.
13. The Presbyterate in Synod, 1866.
14. Hymns for some Sundays and Saints' Days, 1867.
15. Notes on Appendix to Hymns Ancient and Modern, and three
other papers on Hymns in *Literary Churchman*, 1868—9.
16. Essay on Apocalypse in the Bible, with a sketch of an Interpretation of the Apocalypse of St John.   By Pastor Emeritus, 1876.
17. Conciliar Authority for the Mixed Cup in the Holy Eucharist,
1883.

He was the editor of

1. Synodalia, a Journal of Convocation, 1853.
2. The Journal of Convocation, 2 vols., 1855—8.

I have to return my cordial thanks to the Rev. C. F. S. Warren, M.A., of Southfields, Longford, Coventry, the only surviving son of Mr Warren, for his kindness in carefully revising my notes concerning his father, and adding a number of details previously unknown to me.

(XXIV.) JAMES IND SMITH. [1840–1845.]

James Ind Smith was the son of Mr John Smith, of Cambridge, who was University Printer from 1809 to 1836, and was educated at Hingham School, Norfolk, under Mr Browne. He was entered at Trinity College, 9 July, 1831, under Mr Peacock, being then 18 years of age. He was admitted Scholar, 19 April, 1833.

He was awarded the Browne Medal for the Greek and Latin Epigrams in 1834, and that for the Greek Ode in 1835; and the Members' Prize for the Latin Essay in 1835 and 1836. He took the degree of B.A. in 1836 (and was fifth in the First Class of the Classical Tripos), and M.A. in 1839.

He was ordained deacon in 1839, and priest in 1840 by the Bishop of Norwich (Stanley). He was elected Librarian in succession to Mr Warren, 12 March, 1840, and was admitted on July 7 following.

Like his predecessor, he vacated the Librarianship by the acceptance of a living, being presented by the College on 25 April, 1845, to the Vicarage of Marsworth, Bucks., then vacant by the resignation of the Rev. J. Weighall. This he retained till 1847, when on his resignation, the Rev. J. Biass Turner was (Nov. 1) appointed to succeed him.

Mr Smith married Ellen Frances, only daughter of John Temple, Esq., of Malton, Yorkshire. She died 16 Sept. 1887[1]. Mr Smith died 15 Nov. 1896, at Agra Villa, Belmont Hill, Lee, aged 83. He had endowed during his lifetime a pension in connection with the Printers' Pension Association.

---

[1] *Standard* for 16 Sept., 1889.

(XXV.) George Brimley. [1845—1857.]

To the vacancy caused by Mr Smith's acceptance of a living, a new Librarian was appointed, whose name the posthumous publication of his volume of Essays has made familiar to a wide circle of readers.

George Brimley was the son of Mr Augustine Gutteridge Brimley, and was born at Cambridge, 29 Dec. 1819. From the age of eleven to that of sixteen, he was educated at a school at Totteridge, Herts.; and for the next two years he read privately with the Rev. Charles Clayton, Fellow of Caius College. On 5 Feb. 1838, he was entered at Trinity under Mr Whewell (afterwards Master), subsequently passing under Mr J. W. Blakesley (afterwards Dean of Lincoln), on Mr Whewell's resignation of the Tutorship.

He commenced residence in October, 1838, and was admitted Scholar, 23 April, 1841. He read for the Classical Tripos, first under the guidance of the Rev. C. J. Vaughan (then Fellow of the College, afterwards Head Master of Harrow and now Dean of Llandaff) and afterwards with the Rev. Henry Thompson, Fellow of St John's College.

Even at this early period, the malady which ultimately proved fatal had so weakened his constitution, that his chances of success in a competition for honours were seriously affected.

I am informed, moreover, that Mr Brimley had no taste for Mathematics, and this fact had doubtless not a little to do with his not seeking a degree in honours. It will be remembered that it was necessary at that time and for some years afterwards to pass in the Mathematical Tripos as a condition to being allowed to compete in the Classical Tripos.

On the issue of the degree list for 1842, Mr Brimley's name stood 17th in order among those who were not candidates for Honours[1]. He took his B.A. degree in 1842, and M.A. in 1845. During the three intervening years, he took, with considerable success, a large number of private pupils to prepare for College

----

[1] *Cambridge Chronicle* for 22 Jan., 1842.

and University examinations, while continuing his studies with a view to the Fellowship Examination.

. Though he competed twice unsuccessfully, his work impressed the Examiners as being exceedingly good. Through the kindness of Mrs Robert Bowes, Mr Brimley's only surviving sister, I have been permitted to read the testimonials sent in by Mr Brimley on the occasion of a candidature to be presently mentioned. In the general testimonial from the Master and Fellows of Trinity it is remarked that though he was "not elected [Fellow] he impressed the Examiners with a very high idea of his classical attainments and of the elegance of his style of translation." Among individual testimonials from Senior Fellows who had examined Mr Brimley in the Fellowship Examination, Mr Blakesley remarks that he "only just failed to get a Fellowship, and no doubt but for his frequent illnesses he would have got one." Mr J. M. Heath says, "had his Mathematical knowledge been greater than it is, I have little doubt that he would have been successful."

Early in 1845, Mr Brimley was a candidate for the Rectorship of the Ayr Academy and went down on a visit of inspection to Ayr. I have already referred to some of the testimonials sent in connection with this. In addition to these, there are a large number of others all couched in very warm terms. Besides signing the college testimonial, Dr Whewell, then Master, writes a further very cordial little note. Mr Romilly speaks of his "great range of reading coupled with remarkable accuracy." Among others who write are Mr C. J. Vaughan, Mr Carus, and the writer's dear old friend, the late Mr C. W. King.

From a letter which I have been privileged to see, written by Mr Brimley to his father during his visit to Ayr, I gather that while in many ways the post seemed attractive, yet the nature of the work and the conditions of the post were such as did not sufficiently commend themselves to him. It was rather a shock to him, too, with his ideas of English public schools, to find that the Ayr Academy was a mixed school for boys and girls. It would appear that after consultation with his friends at Cambridge he withdrew from his candidature. It cannot be doubted that his health could not long have stood the strain of a schoolmaster's life, and moreover that his literary tastes had a far freer scope amid the comparative leisure of a college life.

He was elected Librarian, 4 June, 1845, and was admitted the same day. From this time forward, the College became his home. He lived in rooms on the corner staircase of the Great Court, by the Master's Lodge, which adjoined the older Library of the College, and indeed had perhaps once formed part of it.

Although Mr Brimley's delicate health stood in the way of his attempting any larger work, such as mental powers like his would naturally have undertaken had bodily strength allowed, still he was able to contribute a number of articles to various literary journals. At a very early period in his career he had written papers for the *Cambridge University Magazine* (1840-3), among these being articles on " Living Dramatists of England," "Poetry, its nature and effect," etc.; while during the later years of his life he wrote regularly for the *Spectator* and occasionally for *Fraser's Magazine*.

All these were published anonymously, the only signed work being, I believe, the long article on Tennyson's Poems, which appeared in the *Cambridge Essays* for 1855, and is apparently the most elaborate piece of work which Mr Brimley left behind him.

His literary work was characterized by a high conscientiousness in the way of careful study of the books he was discussing. It both proved a solace to him in his gradually weakening condition and was the means of bringing him into intimate relations with some of the foremost literary men of the day. Among them was the late Charles Kingsley. In the possession of Mr and Mrs Robert Bowes are a large number of Kingsley's letters, testifying to a warm and intimate friendship between the two men.

Two of these letters are printed in the *Letters and Memories of Charles Kingsley*, edited by his widow[1]. They refer to some correspondence in the *Spectator* on the state of the Universities,

---

[1] Vol. i. pp. 265, 267, ed. 2.

and to Kingsley's belief that "there was a wide-spreading spirit of unbelief among the undergraduates." The second letter thanks Mr Brimley warmly for his "gallant letter" in the *Spectator*.

With Mr F. D. Maurice, too, Mr Brimley was on terms of very warm friendship, and a large number of letters from Mr Maurice to his friend have been preserved.

I am informed that Mr Brimley's most intimate friend, outside the circle of his own family, was certainly the late Mr W. G. Clark, to whose work for his friend I refer subsequently. Mr Clark was with him a few days before his death.

The late Dr Hort was one of Mr Brimley's most intimate friends. In the recently published biography of the former by Mr A. F. Hort, the writer remarks that his father " saw much of George Brimley, whose acute intellect he warmly appreciated," and mentions Brimley's name in the very distinguished body of guests at Hort's " Fellowship dinner[1]." Dr Hort refers to Mr Brimley's Essay on Tennyson to which I have already alluded, in a letter to the Rev. J. Ellerton. He says of the volume of Cambridge Essays, "The gem of it is Brimley's Article on Tennyson, a genuine burst of hearty enthusiasm, ludicrously at variance with all dear Brimley's pet theories (he now professes to believe in nothing but 'nervous tissue'!) and except in one or two groundless cavils, a worthy vindication against the populace[2]."

Another friend with whom Mr Brimley was much thrown was the late Sir Arthur Helps, through their common friendship with Mr J. W. Parker, the publisher.

Amid steadily increasing weakness, but with every solace that the devoted care of his friends could bestow, the last few years of Mr Brimley's life were passed. He died on 29 May, 1857, at his father's house, 13 Park Terrace, and was buried in the Cambridge Cemetery. At the foot of the granite cross above his grave is inscribed the text " Mercy and Truth are met together."

[1] *Life and Letters of F. J. A. Hort*, vol. i. pp. 173—4.
[2] *Ibid.* 320.

In the following year a collection of his Essays was brought out by the late Mr W. G. Clark, then Fellow and Tutor of Trinity, with a short, warmly appreciative memoir.   He concludes with a touching tribute from an unnamed friend, who, I am informed, was Sir Arthur Helps:—"I believe he was an unusually good man, whose goodness was not always prominent to the ordinary observer, but who was intrinsically faithful, true, brave, and affectionate....His death is really a loss to literature.   He was certainly, as it appeared to me, one of the finest critics of the present day.   We shall not soon meet with his like again."

The portrait prefixed to the volume is a steel engraving by E. Radcliffe from a photograph by Mayall, taken in 1856.   It represents a strong intellectual face and withal a pleasant and kindly one.   The family possess also a portrait of Mr Brimley as a young man, painted by Isaac Robert [?] Cruikshank about 1844, and a chalk drawing by A. Ludovici taken about 1850.

There is an error in the life of Mr Brimley in the *Dictionary of National Biography*[1], which states that he retained the Librarianship "until a few weeks before his death."   He was Librarian until his death, as is shewn by the Conclusion which records the election of his successor.   The error is doubtless due to the fact that the last six months of his life were passed not in his college rooms, but at home.   ·

I have to return my best thanks to my friend Mr Bowes for his kind aid in making this notice as accurate as possible.

(XXVI.) HOWARD WARBURTON ELPHINSTONE. [1857—1858.]

To the vacancy caused by the death of Mr Brimley, Mr Howard Warburton Elphinstone was elected.

The new Librarian was the only son of Sir Howard Elphinstone, Bart., was born at Westminster in 1830, and was educated at Eton under Dr Hawtrey.

He was entered at Trinity under Mr (afterwards Archdeacon) Cooper, 4 Feb. 1850, and was admitted Scholar, 9 April, 1853.

---

[1] Vol. vi., p. 344.

He took the degrees of B.A. (as 17th Wrangler) in 1854, and M.A in 1857. He was elected Librarian, 9 June, 1857, and was admitted the following day.

He resigned the Librarianship in the following year, and his successor, Mr John Glover, was appointed on 13 Dec. 1858.

Mr Elphinstone was called to the Bar at Lincoln's Inn in 1862. He was formerly Professor and afterwards Reader of the Law of Real and Personal Property to the Inns of Court. He was appointed Conveyancing Counsel to the Court, Nov. 1895. He succeeded his father as third baronet in 1893.

He is author of

1. A Practical Introduction to Conveyancing, 1871.
   Second edition, 1881.
   Third edition, revised, 1884.
   Fourth edition, 1894.
2. [Jointly with Mr T. Key.] A Compendium of Precedents in Conveyancing, 1878.
   Second edition, 1883.
3. [Jointly with Mr R. F. Norton and Mr James W. Clark.] Rules for the Interpretation of Deeds, 1885.
4. [Jointly with Mr Clark.] On Searches, 1887—9.

(XXVII.) John Glover. [1858—1863.]

John Glover was the son of an officer in the army, John Octavius Glover, who served in the First Royals, and retired from the service as Lieutenant-Colonel. He was born at Waterford, 23 Dec. 1823, and was educated privately in Devonshire.

He was entered at Trinity under Mr Blakesley (afterwards Dean of Lincoln), on 28 June, 1842. He was admitted Scholar, 19 April, 1844, and took the degrees of B.A. (as 18th Wrangler, and 2nd in the Second Class of the Classical Tripos) in 1846 and M.A. in 1849.

He was ordained deacon by the Bishop of Winchester (Sumner) in 1849, and priest by the Bishop of Cork (Wilson) in 1850. He was admitted Chaplain of the College on 29 Oct. 1851, and on 13 Dec. 1858 was elected Librarian on Mr Elphinstone's resignation, and was admitted the same day. He was the last who was sworn on admission ; after Mr Glover's admission, the old "juratus et admissus " becomes " professione facta admissus." The Seniority on 4 March, 1859, allowed Mr Glover to hold his Chaplaincy during a year of Grace.

The Vicarage of Brading, in the Isle of Wight, having become vacant, Mr Glover was presented to it by the college, 1 Dec. 1862. The preliminary formalities evidently took some time, for not till 25 March, 1863, was the vacancy caused by Mr Glover's acceptance of Brading filled up by the election of Mr W. A. Wright.

Mr Glover died on 5 July, 1884, at the house of his brother, the Rev. George Glover, Vicar of Bourton, Dorset, and is buried in the cemetery at Bourton.

Mr Glover was one of the compilers of the *Catalogue of the MSS. in the Library of the University of Cambridge.* His name occurs in vol. I. (1856) as undertaking the scientific and medical MSS., conjointly with Dr Webster of Jesus College. In vols. II. (1857), III. (1858) and IV. (1861) Mr Glover undertook this work alone. In vols. III. and IV. he also took part of the work on the Historical MSS. conjointly with Mr Luard and Mr Ventris.

During this work at the University Library he formed a friendship, which ended only with life, with Professor J. E. B. Mayor and the late Henry Bradshaw.

His name appears as joint editor with Mr W. G. Clark on the title-page of the first volume of the first edition of the Cambridge Shakespeare, 1863 ; but his departure from Cambridge rendered it impossible for him to continue the work of editing, and his place was taken by Mr W. A. Wright. While he was Vicar of Brading, he edited for the Rolls Series, "Le Livere de Reis de Brittanie, e Le Livre de Reis de Engletere," 1865.

I have to thank the Rev. Octavius Glover, B.D., Rector of Emmanuel Church, Loughborough, and formerly Fellow of Emmanuel College, for kindly revising and making some additions to the above details of his brother's life.

(XXVIII.) WILLIAM ALDIS WRIGHT. [1863—1870.]

As I have already said, Mr Wright was appointed to fill the vacancy created by Mr Glover's acceptance of the Vicarage of Brading.

The new Librarian was the son of Mr George Wright, of Beccles in Suffolk, and was educated at the Grammar School there, under the Rev. H. N. Burrows. At the age of 19, he was entered at Trinity under Mr Thompson (afterwards Master), on 6 June, 1850.

He was admitted Scholar, 9 April, 1853; was 18th Wrangler in 1854, and took the degrees of B.A. in 1858 and M.A. in 1861. He was also created Hon. LL.D. at Edinburgh in April, 1879, Hon. D.C.L. at Oxford, 30 June, 1886, and Hon. Litt.D. at Dublin, 28 June, 1895.

He was elected Librarian, 25 March, 1863, and was admitted on May 28 following. He held the Librarianship till appointed Senior Bursar, 9 June, 1870, and held the latter office till December, 1895. He was admitted Fellow, 11 Oct. 1878 [sec. Stat. XXII.], and has been Vice-Master since 3 Feb. 1888.

Mr Wright has published (*inter alia*) the following :—
[as joint-editor with the late Mr W. G. Clark]

1. The first edition of the Cambridge Shakespeare (except vol. I.), 1863—66.

and, as sole editor,

2. The second edition of the above, 1891—93.
3. Bacon's Essays, 1862.
4. „ Advancement of Learning, 1869.
5. [For the Roxburghe Club.] Pilgrimage of the Lyf of the Manhode, an old English prose version of Guillaume de Deguilleville's Pelerinaige de l'homme, 1869.
6. [For the Early English Text Society.] Generydes, a Romance (from the unique MS. of this form of the text in the Gale collection in Trinity College Library), 1873—78.
7. [For the Rolls Series.] The Metrical Chronicle of Robert of Gloucester, 2 vols., 1887.
8. The Bible Word-Book, ed. 2, 1884.
9. Letters and Literary Remains of Edward Fitzgerald, 1889.

10.   Letters of Edward Fitzgerald, 2 vols., 1894.
11.   Letters of Edward Fitzgerald to Fanny Kemble, 1871—83, 1895.

From 1870 to 1885 he was Secretary to the Committee for revising the Authorised Version of the Old Testament.

(XXIX.) SEDLEY TAYLOR. [1870—1871.]

On Mr Wright's appointment as Senior Bursar he was succeeded as Librarian by Mr Sedley Taylor. The new Librarian was the son of Mr George Taylor, of Kingston, Surrey, and received his school education, first at Hofwyl under De Fellenberg, and afterwards at the school attached to University College, London. He subsequently attended lectures at that College, especially those of Professor De Morgan, and took the degree of B.A. at the University of London. At the age of 20, he was entered at Trinity under Mr Cooper, 8 Jan. 1855, and was admitted Scholar, 25 April, 1857. He took the degrees of B.A. (as 16th Wrangler) in 1859 and M.A. in 1862.

He was admitted Fellow, 11 Oct. 1861, and was elected and admitted Librarian, 9 June, 1870, but resigned the Librarianship in the May following in consequence of illness. Mr Taylor has published the following:

1.   The so-called "Real objective Presence" in the Lord's Supper no doctrine of the Church of England. A letter to the Author of the "Kiss of Peace," 1867.

2.   The system of Clerical subscriptions in the Church of England; its unjustifiable character and injurious results examined, 1869.

3.   On French and German as substitutes for Greek in the University Pass examinations, 1870.

4.   Sound and Music: a non-Mathematical Treatise on the Physical Constitution of Musical Sounds and Harmony, 1873.

5.   The conduct of Her Majesty's Ministers on the Eastern question, 1877.

6.   The Earl of Beaconsfield and the Conservative Reform Bill of 1867, 1877.

7.   Memoranda extracted from the correspondence respecting Afghanistan, 1878.

8.   The Participation of Labour in the Profits of Enterprise, 1881.

9. What results may be expected to arise from an Extension of the system of Participation by Labour in the Profits of Manufacturing, Agricultural, and Trading Enterprises, 1881.

10. The Tonic Sol-Fa movement: what it is, and why Rich and Poor should alike support it, 1883.

11. The late R. C. Rowe, formerly Fellow (*In memoriam*), 1884.

12. Inaugural Address delivered at the sixteenth Annual Co-operative Congress held at Derby, June 2—4, 1884, 1884.

13. Profit-Sharing between Capital and Labour, to which is added a Memorandum on the Industrial Partnership at the Whitwool Collieries (1865—1874). Together with remarks on the Memorandum, 1884.

14. The Minor Notation of the Tonic Sol-Fa system. A paper read at the Association of Tonic Sol-Fa Choirs, Feb. 26, 1887.

15. A System of Sight-Singing from the Established Musical Notation, based on the Principles of Tonic Relation, 1890.

16. The "Substantial" and "Wave" Theories of Sound. Two letters by A. Wilford Hale and Sedley Taylor, 1891.

17. A Record of the Cambridge Centennial Commemoration, on Dec. 4 and 5, 1891, of Wolfgang Amadé Mozart. Edited by Sedley Taylor, 1892.

(XXX.) ROBERT SINKER. [1871.]

The present Librarian is the son of the late Mr Robert Sinker, of Liverpool, and was educated at Liverpool College, under Dr Howson, afterwards Dean of Chester. At the age of 19, he was entered at Trinity, under Mr Mathison (afterwards Vice-Master), 15 Jan. 1858.

He was admitted Scholar, 13 April, 1861; and took the degrees of B.A. 1862, M.A. 1865, B.D. 1880, D.D. 1890. He was elected a corresponding member of the Royal Bohemian Society of Sciences (Prague) 8 Jan. 1890.

He was ordained deacon in 1863 by Bishop Turton of Ely, and priest in 1864 by Bishop Harold Browne of Ely. He was admitted Chaplain on 10 July, 1865; was elected Librarian, 2 June, 1871, and admitted on Oct. 13 following.

He has published:—

1. The Testaments of the XII. Patriarchs; an Attempt to estimate their Historic and Dogmatic Worth: together with the text of the Cambridge MS. and the various readings of the Oxford MS., 1869.

2.   Appendix to above, with collation of the Roman and Patmos MSS. and Bibliographical Notes, 1879.

3.   Catalogue of the Fifteenth-Century Printed Books in the Library of Trinity College, Cambridge, 1876.

4.   Catalogue of Books printed before 1601, now in the Library of Trinity College, Cambridge, 1885.

5.   Memorials of the Hon. Ion Keith-Falconer, 1888.

6.   The Psalm of Habakkuk, 1890.

7.   The Library of Trinity College, Cambridge, 1891.

He has also written many Calendar and Vestment articles in Smith and Cheetham's *Dictionary of Christian Antiquities* (1875—80), and one of the Essays in *Lex Mosaica* (1894); and has edited Pearson's *Exposition of the Creed* for the Syndics of the University Press.

INDEX.

CAMBRIDGE: PRINTED BY J. AND C. F. CLAY, AT THE UNIVERSITY PRESS.